MW00413489

The Scream
&
Other Dark Stories

written by Jerry Sampson
&
illustrated by Sean Croghan

Buckman Publishing LLC
PO Box 14247
Portland OR 97293
buckmanpublishing.com

The Scream and Other Dark Stories/ Jerry Sampson

ISBN: 9781733724531
Library of Congress Control Number: 2020948434

Book design by Hannah Johnson

We are a river to our people.

to Trask,
my ideas guy

contents

mirrors 1

the lifetime channel 9

abigail alone 19

the metal box 29

razor, rope, retribution, release 37

to everything, turn 49

mathias & LEENA 59

donuts once a year 71

dandelions in the forest 79

black wings 87

amphibiman 97

the only thing to do 105

come on up to the house 115

the scream 123

"T'ain't no sin to take off your skin
And dance around in your bones."

— Tom Waits

I.

mirrors

My mother took down the mirrors after catching me putting lipstick on before a school dance. I thought she left for work, so my guard was down and my headphones on and I didn't hear her as she slipped back into the house for her final once-over.

She was so furious at me for applying *whore's blood* to my lips that she near cut my face off when she shoved it into the glass of the mirror. Shards stuck into my cheek and lip as my mother screamed a litany of reprimands and sharp curses. I saw through my one unaffected eye that she was crying as she used her sleeve to sop up the blood, but her words were cutting and mean; like a husband's declaration of *I wish you wouldn't make me do this to you* after he slaps a steak on the cheek he bruised.

After that, as if my mangled face wasn't punishment enough, she took the mirrors off the walls. While she stitched my open, seeping signs of disobedience, she told me it'd be a miracle of God if she didn't get right fired from work for having to miss her shift. I toyed with the idea of choosing that moment to tell her I didn't believe in no God who'd stick me in a home with such a monster as she, but my right mind took control and I kept my eyes down and my swollen mouth shut.

I wondered what she thought of me, to believe that I'd be gutted over the removal of a couple of mirrors.

Taking the time through the white noise of my mother's verbal lashing, I thought back to the first signs of her capacity for cruelty.

It was a week past my 11th birthday, and an hour past the start of my first period.

She used to read books to me before bed. Prior to that day, we went to Tex-Mex every Sunday after church as a special treat. She'd drink two margaritas, and I'd go in the back to help the cooks make a fried dough dessert. I'm pretty sure she loved me then.

The day of my first period, my father took off on us and I guess I became my mother's worst enemy. I could feel the shift in the air, as if a heavy dusting of chemical hatred was wafting over the whole house and settling on me; everything that I touched and ate and looked at became fair game. Especially those mirrors. In the morning I'd brush my teeth in front of the bathroom mirror and could feel her staring at me from the doorway, but I'd never look. Like a monster in the corner that doesn't exist until you give it a glance, I kept my eyes closed while I brushed my hair and washed my face. I couldn't understand why she was acting so strange and I couldn't ask her, so I pretended it was all in my imagination. Playing pretend was my avoidance, and I did so well enough, until well enough no longer held its weight.

Soon, my mother removed the door to the bathroom to be able to monitor me during my time of the month. I used techniques gleaned from magazines that I snuck into my cardigan at the checkout counter, to soak up the blood that I was certain was so dark because I was dying. Her lips curled into constant sneers as she scoffed at my fumbling attempts to apply the pad to my underpants, having to stick and un-stick it over and over to get it lined up right. I learned soon enough to forget about privacy around my mother.

I remained hopeful for a time that my father would return. I knew in my heart that leaving was the only way he could save himself, but I felt sure that he would find a way to save me, too. After a whole year went by without a word from him, I realized that I was a sacrifice made by my father to rid himself of my mother.

My mother's favorite pastime was playing the "Blame Game",

wherein she'd tell me all the reasons my father left me. Her denial was in full effect and I knew no better so I believed her. She insisted that my father couldn't handle the smell of my blood, that a man could never resist a girl-woman and my ascent into womanhood prompted my father's descent into betrayal. The books she once read me were replaced with tales of his galivanting about with girls barely legal, all to satisfy the needs that my maturation had cursed him with.

My mother knew my cycle, and each new month she was relentless as she explained how male animals rape females while they're in heat due to the uncontrollable nature of mammals. She reminded me that men are mammals, too. I hated how poetic she attempted to make her cruelty sound as she illustrated the creative ways men find to creep into a girl's panties.

My mother only got worse as my hair grew longer and my breasts larger. I could practically see the venom coursing through her veins, particularly the one that protruded from her forehead as she berated me nightly. I dreamt about cutting that vein just as it jutted as far as it would go, washing my mother's face in her own blood and leaving her to die, but I never dared, sure that she'd only find some other, otherworldly way to haunt me instead.

On the night of my sixteenth birthday, my mother shaved my head. Her hands shook as she roughly dragged the electric razor through my long hair, yanking the tough pieces out when they got stuck, ignoring my cries. Earlier, as I was dressing for dinner, she caught me gazing at my reflection in the hallway mirror. I swore on her life that I was only working out a tangle, and she took my wrist in her bloated fingers and pulled me into the bathroom. *No daughter of mine* she muttered over and over again. *Vanity, impurity, vanity, lust, no daughter of mine.* Over and over she spat the words, a confirmation of every suspicion she ever had about me.

My only two friends at school stopped talking to me after I arrived with a chop-shop mop-top that Monday. They'd forgotten my birthday anyways and weren't very nice to me, but at least they let me sit with them and talk about boys. They said they were too embarrassed to be around me and that everyone was talking about me behind my back. I wish I could have told them to shove off, but years of keeping my mouth shut continued to serve me not so well.

With the laughter of my entire class trailing behind me, I ran off to the woods behind the school and decided to be done with it all.

Kneeling beside the small creek littered with used condoms and baby wipes, I got set to drown myself. Being the dead of winter, I felt that if I couldn't stand holding my head under that nasty water, I'd at least die of hypothermia if I stuck my bald head in and waited.

Just as I steeled my will enough to really make the move, I heard a rustling to my left, followed by a deep, guttural growling that reminded me of an old horror movie my father once took me to when I was a kid. As the growling intensified, I began to shake, feeling small as any little girl facing her monster. I wanted to run, to hide, scream, cower. All the things that I learned to do to avoid my fear, but something about that moment really turned on me.

No, it really turned me on.

The shaking in my body was letting loose a part of me that was locked up, got locked up the day my father left, the day my mother became my villain. I trembled, not from the cold, but from the warmth that was growing deep down in my belly and extending to both ends of my body.

The growling stopped soon, but I didn't.

I picked myself up. I stormed back to school. I raised hell with my two ex-friends, and then I asked a boy to the dance that night, and he said yes.

Later that night, as she stitched up my face, I stopped looking down. I stared. Defiant in my fury. She didn't know the half of what I could do. My anger burrowed through me and came out of every pore, I knew she could smell it.

In that moment, for the first time, I faced my demon straight on, and I saw fear in my mother's eyes. †

II.

the lifetime channel

MARY ELLEN BEGAN HER WALK in an attempt to clear her head of the cobwebs that family often covered her with. She continued involuntarily, with a knife pressed to her back and a cloth over her face; she didn't realize that her freedom was taken from her until it had been gone for hours — maybe days.

She awoke in a dark room, her head a splitting melon unable to formulate a concise thought, let alone piece together the events that led her there.

***

Pardon, do you have a cigarette? The voice came from nowhere and disarmed her with its deep, British lilt.

No, she didn't smoke. Sorry. But it didn't end there. When she looked towards the voice, she was apprehended from behind. A team effort. One of them devastatingly handsome and the other – the other she never saw coming.

With a cloth over her face, she drifted to sleep.

***

One hand was suspended over her head, and Mary Ellen realized that she couldn't wiggle her fingers, the blood having washed through her veins, resting in a pool inside her shoulder. All her attacker would need to do was prick that spot with a needle and she'd bleed out. What a way to go.

With the other hand, Mary Ellen felt the surrounding space. She was able to touch a wall behind her, one to the side, and the rest was a dark chasm of the unknown.

She thought about her mother, the reason for the escape from one home and subsequent entrapment in another. Mary Ellen felt sure that after they found her body the real circus would begin. At her Shiva her mother would fling her arms high in the air as gnashing and wailing commenced. She'd open an eye every now and again, to make sure she held her audience, and then proceed.

I always told her! I taught her! Never to go with strangers!

The irony of it all would be lost on her mother, that if you only teach a girl to fear, she may just enter her own world with a sense of nihilistic trust.

They can't all be that bad, as bad as my crazy mother says.

And thus, they'll seal her coffin.

Mary Ellen was certain that she'd die in that space; within the dark and the dank. She could smell the mold, and amidst the silence was sure she heard the spores pulsing through the air, spinning around her before being *sucked* into her pores. If her kidnapper didn't kill her, then the blackness attaching itself to her lungs most definitely would.

She wished she could see. Anything at all would be better than the nothingness that she faced. She didn't care even if it was a pile of dead bodies; if there was blood on the walls and rats at her feet, she'd take it, she'd deal with it. Anything would be better.

She quickly brought her free hand to her face, overwhelmed with the thought that perhaps she'd been blinded. Was she drugged and enucleated? If a man can capture, then he may have no issue with maiming. She breathed a sigh of relief when her fingers traced two very prominent bulbs. Her eyes were what drew people to her the most. Mary Ellen would get stares as she walked down the street, as people gazed into the amber-colored abyss; the two things that her mother passed along that didn't cause her grief. Her huge, cartoon princess eyes managed to distract from her large nose and too-tight curls. She would have been devastated to find them missing.

With that concern set aside, Mary Ellen was able to think.

A shuffling sound cut the silence and she lifted her head, cocking it as though the small lift in the elevation of her right ear would open some extra channels. It was footsteps, followed by muffled voices – men, at least two of them. Mary Ellen felt like a detective solving her own case and almost smiled. For a moment she wondered if she should call out. Perhaps if she could get them to just turn a light on; she'd be grateful to sacrifice a couple of minutes of torture for a clear view of where she was. The morbid curiosity was killing her.

She thought also of those shows her mother let her watch when she was a kid, the ones on the Lifetime Channel, that showed teenagers getting abducted and then inexplicably falling in love with their captors. The shows always ended in a death and a lesson, but before she was abducted, she was definitely interested in one of her captors. When she put her mind to it, she couldn't figure a time that she ever suspected an attractive person of nefarious intentions. She vowed that if she got out of those chains and that mess that she'd go out of her way to fight the threat of beauty.

A door to her left and high up opened, and a light shone briefly on a long flight of stairs.

A basement. Of course.

The mystery was solved, and Mary Ellen instantly felt better. That little bit of light gave her hope, like she imagined her mother must feel about faith and that whole grift. She never attached herself to theology, but didn't begrudge her mother her beliefs; she always treated Mary Ellen better after synagogue anyways, so why press the issue?

A pair of boots descended the stairs and the hope that had filled Mary Ellen deflated. If there was one thing she knew, it was that the moment she saw her captor's face, she'd be a goner. Death certificate signed. No hope left. She quickly shut her eyes, just in case the man hadn't decided to kill her yet.

"You can open your eyes."

Mary Ellen shook her head from side to side, flexing her shackled hand to remind it that it's still attached.

"Mary Ellen, open your eyes."

Her name. How did he know her name? Now she was really itching with curiosity, but she still kept her eyes shut.

"Have it your way. I'm not going to hurt you."

She didn't believe him; he already had hurt her; her head was throbbing.

Should I try to convince him that I already love him? Or wait until after he starts undressing me?

All the episodes came rushing back to her. She didn't have so much pride that she'd sacrifice her life for her body.

The man sat heavily beside her, and soon she felt his hand on her wrist.

Here we go, Mary Ellen, you be strong now.

Expectations upturned, he merely began unlocking the cuff around her wrist. Her hand, with a life of its own, dropped to her lap. She rubbed the tender skin and held her breath, anticipating the scalpel sinking easily into her skin, the sadistic phlebotomy was nigh.

"Damn it all to hell. Your mom is a real piece of work."

Mary Ellen bristled.

"What does my mom have to do with this?" She demanded more than asked.

She kept her eyes closed as the man stood and crooked a hand around her elbow, pulling her to her feet.

"You should know that she refused even a discounted price for your release."

Her legs took a second to get re-accustomed to standing, and the pins really started poking her arm; long, thick needles traveling straight through from one side to another.

"I mean, we're no killers, but she can't know that."

The man obviously overestimated her mother.

"So, I'd suggest you figure that out. She was ready to say adios. I mean, you live with her, right? Damn. I thought my mom was fucked up. You should really get out of her house."

Mary Ellen wondered if that was an invitation.

She let the man guide her up the stairs, eyes still shut tight. The man muttered a few more words, obviously disappointed in the outcome of his ill-advised plan. After a stumble or two, he put her in a car and she listened to a popular song on the radio as he drove her away from wherever she was held.

When Mary Ellen was found later that day on the side of the road, one wrist bruised badly but the rest of her all well and good, her mother accused her of playing a prank. At one point she turned the whole ordeal around to show how badly she, saintly mother of a devilish imp, felt victimized by Mary Ellen's *nonsense.*

Mary Ellen didn't expect her mother to cry for her, but was not happy at the implication that she'd work that hard just to make her mad.

At the end of the ordeal, Mary Ellen took the man's suggestion, packed up a few belongings, and took off on the Amtrak in the middle of the night. She knew that she'd just be reinforcing her mother's suspicion, but she didn't care. If she felt safer ensnared in a sinister plan of kidnapping and bribery than in her own home, then she needed to seriously reconsider her situation.

And so, she did. Mary Ellen reconsidered it all the way out of town, with her eyes closed tight, waiting to be surprised by wherever she ended up. †

III.

abigail alone

IN A MATTER OF FIVE MINUTES Abigail lost her best friend. Seven minutes past that her husband followed. They were dropping like flies. The threads that she so strongly relied upon to hold her world together unraveled far quicker than they took to secure, and the confusion on her face must have been plain. Still, neither stayed to make sure Abigail was okay. They were done with her just as they began with each other.

The taste of betrayal stuck in the back of her throat, impossible to swallow or wash down, no matter the devices she enlisted to help try. The liquor cabinet was her first victim, a gentleman from the bar her next. There's no accounting for taste when you are mourning a loss so great it tears your insides out. It's like viewing the world through blood-stained glasses, a morbid and macabre viewfinder that directs your attention from one pitiful memory to the next.

She spit and clawed and raced through each phase of grief as though she were given a free get-out-of-sadness punch card that expired soon. No one was watching as she threw caution to the wind. No comfort, but also no judgement; none but for her eyes, staring back at her in the mirror after particularly raucous nights of late-thirties partying and early-twenties screwing.

As time trudged by, Abigail looked at the posts on social media, the details of her husband's new love, the happiness that her best friend found. They filtered and flittered their way across every platform, rubbing her face in their soulmate status. One night, way late and several drinks deep, she posted her own passive aggressive status update:

In A Relationship
with
George Clooney's Fucking Tequila

The morning after, along with a wicked hangover and unyielding shame, Abigail was forced to figure out how to delete a post that she really felt was funny at the time, but of course was a mistake. Two hours and a phone call to her mother later, she threw her hands up and cancelled all her social media accounts. She didn't figure her ninety followers would miss her; the lady cuckold, the fool.

There was no book to prepare her for such tremendous emptiness. Some people gracefully fall into the darkness and come out shiny and new.

Others fall and fall and continue on like that.

***

A month and a day after venturing back into the world alone, Abigail discovered something about herself she was certain was buried way deep down. She felt so hard, so painfully hard, for those thirty-one days, that what she discovered was her innate ability to shut the well off for good and for all once it reached the level marked "FULL". She never noticed the small dots and dashes that covered her inside and out, a Morse code of dreams and failures, ledgers of manic episodes and periods of elation. One lover, the youngest, dragged his fingers across her belly and arms, giggling strangely as he spoke of Braille and his mother and how she went blind. Abigail couldn't shake him off but also couldn't bear to hear his story as he blathered on and on. It reminded her of her husband, except she couldn't get enough when her husband spoke.

After unearthing the scar tissue she wallpapered over when her father died, Abigail no longer felt anything at all. She saw the wounds that healed, opened, and healed again, but could not remember what caused them. At night, Abigail cut the wires keeping her jaw clenched shut; in the morning, the headaches were worse and her voice hoarse from screaming. The scars were floodgates and she wondered when exactly they had been built.

Pain was replaced by determination. She needed to feel. But the skin held strong as she scraped blade after blade over it. The blonde blade was dull, the redheaded one too needy. The blades all wanted to talk after their failed attempt to penetrate. They wished for a story to lull them to sleep after realizing that only one body would come that night.

Abigail's aggression grew. She began calling her husband every night, after the drink but before the fall. The keloids that formed over the forgotten pain were ugly and pulsed in the moonlight, and Abigail was certain there was a door open that only her husband could close. But when she called, her best friend answered, her voice a cold sheet covering Abigail's sweat-wet body. She knew that her husband was there, in the background, a grumbling baritone of sleep-stained speech; her best friend lied as she hung up before Abigail could yell out to him.

The fissure would begin in her mind, deep inside where she kept her darkness. From there it would spread, like lava seeps through a volcano's vent; fiery veins opening and swallowing the animals and the earth and her joy.

***

It was two months and five days since Abigail had been left, broken and beaten and eaten and scabbed. Her house reeked of stale tears and bodies. The stench of bodies could not be denied, rotten meat that the dog wouldn't eat.

In the corner, Abigail sketched her new story. Scratching it into the last of the wall space.

Even her back was marked. Not every lover cared about her well-being and comfort. When she begged, some of them would take the small knife she held out to them and eliminate bits of her anguish.

She assured them it was a pleasure-thing, and they squeezed her as blood pooled in tiny puddles around their writhing bodies.

She stopped calling her husband, and only dreamt of wriggling in her best friend's skin.

She decided to spare them after plotting went sideways. One plan felt amateurish and forced, and Abigail quickly disposed of the strange man who proposed it.

He was, in fact, at the bottom of the pile. Her first, the musician from the train. He never questioned as she led him where he needed to be, in that house, following his pleasure as men do and do and always will; and he lay with his eyes wide and mouth gaping, as she writhed over him, scars moving across her body like a picture show.

It was easiest the first time, as the blade was sharper than ever. So much easier than watching her own skin resist and pull tight before finally releasing its tissue to the steel.

At last, she felt. With that first man, more than ever. And she made certain that he felt nothing, because the last thing she wanted was a survivor's struggle; by that time, she was a mere wisp of a woman, and her body wouldn't hold against strong hands.

As Abigail felt more, it became harder. The numbing agent that her loneliness spread over her was fading. She was in a place too dark to see but for a pinprick of light, and too wet to climb, for the walls stretched high and melted to her touch.

She chased her grief with a shot of sex and a lick of blood. Sometimes she'd crawl over the bodies as the stack grew, playing at feeling like a wolf.

Abigail wasn't meant to be alone. Her father used to lock her away from the rest of the family when she'd do something bad, and her only recourse was to carve her friends into her arms using the splinters she'd peel from the wood of the closet door. She taught herself to forget about her father; using a whole roll of wallpaper to smother her memories.

***

One year in, Abigail jumped from the roof and landed on her face. She didn't die, but she'd never lure a lover in the same old way again. The doctors needed to cut her clothes off to pump her stomach and patch her wounds. But they couldn't find the new scrapes from the old to determine which were mendable. Her face was a broken bone, her body was a Jackson Pollock painting, chaotic but alluring. The doctors didn't fix her, but they tended to what they could, and stood to the side with their arms crossed when the cops took space outside her room.

When her husband and best friend came, Abigail was chained to the bed and in the middle of a fitful sleep. She thrashed, nearly breaking the bones in her wrist to match the rest of her. The nurses stopped running to her bedside days before, bored of her desperate attempts for attention. Her best friend stood back, in a corner, cloaked in shadows. When Abigail finally awoke, she saw her best friend and was sure she was Death. That calmed her down.

Abigail's husband wiped the sweat from her brow; a tender gesture that refueled her hope. He was quick to remind her of who she had become. Asked her about the disease, about the bodies, about the clocks and gashes and pictures on the wall. She felt the pressure rise, boiling in her skin; the lava flowed and veins pulsed. In a low voice, Abigail pleaded for him to come closer, he owed her that if nothing else. He told her not to touch him and she flinched so hard that a stitch in her eye split. Her husband's lip curled in disgust.

All Abigail saw was red.

***

There was a funeral for her mom, a wedding for her husband, and Abigail was back on the wagon. A forced realization that it could only be the booze that caused such graphic hallucinations. Her face was mostly healed, and she reveled in the thought of keeping one side of her face for lovers and the other side to scare the wretched kids on the third floor.

Gloves glued over her hands kept Abigail from splitting open her skin or gouging out her eyes. The space in which she slept was small enough to feel contained and soft enough to keep her from bashing her brains in. No one prepared her for the comedown. And while Abigail was never meant to be alone, she could not bear the thought of sharing her space with another. Loneliness was the only way for Abigail. If anyone approached her, she'd burn their skin, so better to lock her up. She'd find a way to ruin them, so better to — †

IV.

the metal box

KATY AWOKE IN THE DARK, SKIN STICKY, throat a raw tunnel; she must have been screaming in her sleep. Moving her hands, the most she could make out was metal – a metal box, suffocating. As far as she could tell, she was alone there. Her skin didn't touch skin, breath didn't join breath. Alone.

And naked.

With horror, she realized she was stark naked and sitting on a thin patch of cloth. It protected her from nothing, yet she felt grateful for it.

Grateful?

What a strange word to cross her mind. She felt utterly abandoned by the god she always trusted. A crude laugh escaped her lips, like an unexpected belch, and she felt inclined to cover her mouth and apologize.

For a moment, Katy entertained the idea that she was the subject of a prank. One of her American friends would open the invisible latch, the light shining in and blinding her, laughter and champagne greeting her from above or below – depending on where the latch was fixed. But as her hands moved along the metal more urgently, she knew that was a fool's fantasy.

It was smooth; no seam, no hinge. Like a coffin soldered from within. The perfect trap to keep someone in, keep the world out.

Katy took a second to be still and listen. It was so quiet she could hear her heartbeat echo through the box. She scolded her heart and told it to *shush*, the way her mother once did when she brought Katy with her to the factory.

Not a squeak, little mouse, the cat will hear you and pounce…

She palmed the tears that started to fall and licked her hand. All at once, there was a loud scraping. The noise turned into a slide of metal against wood and Katy felt a heavy weight hit her shin. She reached down and quickly found what struck her. She lifted it up, moved it around in her hand. It was familiar.

Brrrrr...CRACK. A billiard ball. Something from one of her father's games.

"Will you play with me?" The child's voice cut through the silence like a scalpel.

Icicles slid up Katy's spine; air sucked from her lungs. She couldn't speak.

"Did you find my ball? It won't bounce, but we can still play."

It was a girl with a soft and shaky cadence. Katy leaned forward in the dark, hands reaching out, both hopeful and fearful of touching skin. There was nothing. Even as she rose onto her knees, no longer held by that scrap of cloth, she was certain that hers was the only warm body in the space.

"Why am I here?" The child pleaded; the purest form of fear Katy ever heard. She sat back and wrapped her arms around her chest. She was overcome with a freezing chill, brought on by an impossible breeze.

The metal box jolted, moaned –

Water.

She felt a sudden wave of nausea and wretched. There was nothing in her stomach, so the heave was dry and excruciating on her esophagus, which desperately needed water. Katy passed a hand over her face and sopped up the tears that came, drank what little she could gather.

The box jolted once more, and yet again, and soon Katy found a sort of solace in the rocking. She lifted her head and looked forward into the inky darkness.

"My name is Katy," she whispered, "and I am lost here."

A breath sailed through on another breeze and hit Katy as a putrid wall.

"I'm lost here, too." The girl's sadness filled the metal box with an oppressive humidity, and any clean air it held quickly evaporated. Katy lifted her hand and covered her mouth and nose.

"You don't have time, Katharina." The child sounded different.

It was her mother's voice, and it filled the space, using the name Katy abandoned when she came to America. *Katharina, little mouse, the cat has caught you.*

The metal box lurched and tilted before coming to a shuddering halt. Outside the box, the tinny voice of a man, just one man.

"You only have one chance." The girl's voice rang in Katy's ear.

She clutched the billiard ball, pushing it into her palm until it hurt. The man's muffled voice stopped; Katy thought he must have been speaking into a phone. The box vibrated. Soon, she began to see sparks of light, felt her skin burn as flame bit through the metal.

She shielded her eyes as gloved hands pried the box open. Katy adjusted to the light and saw him, leering, eyes watering and hungry as he leaned in.

You only have one chance. Katy heard without hearing.

She thrust her palm up with every ounce of strength she had, and somehow so much more. The billiard ball hit the man square in the nose, shattering bones into his skull.

He fell back without a sound.

Katy was blinded. She waited for another attacker, but none came. She began to acclimate, her eyes adjusting to the sun beating down on her naked body. Once able, she looked at her metal coffin. It was a shipping container painted to look like wood on the outside. A packing crate for American goods being sent overseas.

In the space across from where she was curled, the body of a girl, long dead, was bound and gagged.

Katy cried. She cried for the girl, and cried to the girl, and let the girl cry to her. When she was finished, she picked the girl up and thanked her, then carried her to the water, and gently set her free. †

V.

razor, rope, retribution, release

YOU KNOW I JUST REALIZED, I WHISPERED INTO THE DARK, that I'd rather feel any other emotion than sadness. And then I stepped off the rafter and felt my body for the first time, before the *snap* and blackness took hold. I'm pretty sure that when they found me, I was smiling.

***

But before that night, I was a coyote, stalking the LA streets.

I stomped through the lives of my actors, channeling their angry father or alcoholic mother. I did anything I needed to get the performance, neglecting the fact that they were only first-year students, hungry to learn from me; all I gave them was abuse fueled by envy and an innate sense of wrath, forged in the fires of years of rejection. My lust for art and the stage had broken me. And so, I was determined to inflict the same pain on the beauties who stumbled through rehearsals and opening night. My vitriol convinced me that they deserved every bit of takedown that I offered.

They. What did *they* know of life and pain? With their leased Mercedes, cocaine-fueled perfect bodies, pearly white teeth and unscorched hearts. It was my job to guide them past their charmed existence and into the depths of the human experience, to really capture the acting craft.

Mostly, the kids stared at me with enamored slack jaws. They were told that I was the best. I didn't adjust the fables toward truth, and let my students hold me to the high expectations they didn't even have for their preachers and parents. I hated them for believing without seeing, but reminded myself that they were fetuses, newly conceived in the industry. I'd wait for their messy births at the hands of lecherous producers on filthy leather couches to brand them as I've been branded.

***

It was hours before I was cut down. My eyes were fixed in a gaze, looking out upon my final audience. The vessels in my eyes had broken, and I shed at least one tear of blood. It made for a dramatic post-mortem picture; I almost wished they'd use it for my obituary page but was certain that my twenty-year-old head shot would be chosen for that honor.

Those were the last professional pictures I took and, admittedly, the last marketable time of my life. As a brand, I went downhill fast. Refusing to adhere to the blowhard demands of Hollywood, my anti-Botox/plastic surgery stance was really the first platform from which I hung. There was no honor in aging gracefully for working actresses; we couldn't all mature like Nicole Kidman.

But in death, I digress…

***

Mary Elizabeth first stepped into the theater on a rare rainy LA day. When the sky opened in SoCal, the world may as well have ended; no one knows left from right when the weather turns. I grew up in Oregon, where rain soaked my bones nine months out of the year. My memories of winter were of wringing out my hair on the hardwood floors before getting hit upside the head by my overweight and overbearing mother, screamed at to shake off outside like a dog.

The girl was nineteen. A baby. With a baby face and baby-fine hair that floated around her like a greasy halo. She was different than any other young ingénue who practiced their graceful gait and sly half-moon smile. Mary Elizabeth was a bumpkin, a Pollyanna, the point driven home the second she opened her mouth and uttered her first *y'all.*

I was inexplicably intoxicated. I'd of course enjoyed my share of elicit encounters in the theater. The lithe bodies of the twenty-something boys and girls flittered in and out of my bed. I promised them nothing and they gave me everything. But it wasn't until Mary Elizabeth that I paused to think I could ever find actual happiness.

***

I wanted to scream, watching the pretty girls weep in the corner.

"I've never seen a dead *body* before."

"Omg, is it illegal to snapchat a dead body?"

"Ms. Erica would want us to use these feelings for the performance tonight."

I hated it when they called me Ms. Erica.

I emphasized on the first day of class that I was to be called Erica; not Ms. Erica, not Ms. Tannabourne, just Erica.

Like Prince, or Cher.

The bitches disrespected me even as my dead body succumbed to rigor mortis ten feet away. I felt it as it happened; I wish I could have known that feeling in life, it would have been so useful during my year of writing, to have really known the sensation of death. It's useless to me now.

***

Mary Elizabeth earned a scholarship for a year of my theater classes by writing an essay in high school. I remember reading it and rolling my eyes, as I did at every essay that every teenager ever wrote…ever. I simply couldn't stand the drivel; they hadn't lived enough to deserve a voice. But in order to keep the funds coming from the great state of California, I was obligated to participate in the scholarship program. And to be honest, it helped that each essay came with an audition video; a real proper way to weed out the undesirables.

It was in the video that I saw the potential of Mary Elizabeth. Her writing was simple, unaffected, but her eyes portrayed something entirely different. Those dark brown eyes with the embers of fire burning through. Those eyes had seen some shit.

And so, it is with great joy, I extend to you, Mary Elizabeth Collins, the 2018 Tannabourne Acting Fellowship. Accommodations and airfare not included.

And it really was with great joy. The days leading up to the new semester I found myself growing excited. It was a confusing time because, in all honesty, I didn't want to have sex with her. I didn't want to talk to her about her life. I just wanted to be in her presence. Confounding. And not just that, but inspiring. I watched her tape over and over, meditating on the monotonous drone of her voice, tinged with insecurity. After, I'd sit down with a timer to write for an hour and three hours later would close my laptop and light a cigarette, breathing heavily as I would after a rousing afternoon of fucking.

When the day of her arrival finally came, I had an almost paralyzing fear that her physical presence would scrap all of my mental metal, but I needn't worry; she stepped through those doors and I fell completely in love. But not just that, not just love, but the first love that I ever really, truly felt. After two failed marriages and hundreds of naked bodies pressed against me, it was this teenager who unveiled love for me.

***

I listened as the police questioned each student separately, not ruling out some sort of lover's quarrel or eager actor's crime of passion. But they all had their alibis. Young and beautiful people in LA never spend a night alone.

Most of them confirmed my miserable temperament and told the cops that they assumed it was good old-fashioned suicide. That was what the cop was afraid of, because that made it two suicides in less than a week. And there's no pretty bow to tie that case up with. Not to mention the publicity, my being a popular figure in the Hollywood theater scene. It was more than the officials wanted to deal with and, on my end, I was ready for them to finish up so that I could start my afterlife journey. I had plans, after all.

***

It didn't take long to guess Mary Elizabeth's past, her spotty family history; abuse, addiction, little bouts of aggression and violence. It was a common theme in the young ones who run off to Tinseltown. Too beautiful to stay in rural bum-fuck America, too innocent to survive the entertainment biz. Kids like her were chewed up and swallowed by the city; I directed at least three a semester at the theater. Usually I didn't step in or impose. But Mary Elizabeth needed me more than the others, even if she didn't know it.

I offered her a room above the main hall, something I absolutely never did and that she must absolutely never mention. She agreed, excited and practically drooling with appreciation. I could have probably had her then, but I was still uncertain as to whether that was the intention of my love-feelings. Sex brought out a part of me that I wasn't proud of; a certain devilish and sadistic aspect to my otherwise charming demeanor. *Indeed.* And so, I assured her that there were no strings to our arrangement, I wanted only to see her rise to her potential. I think I may have been the first woman to believe in her.

At the beginning of the semester I didn't show any favoritism. I knew better. The competition coming out of the theater was intense and I'd seen how cruel young actors could be when they felt threatened. But when I introduced Mary Elizabeth to a casting agent friend, and she got her first audition, there were three girls in class that heard about it. I couldn't help it once it got out. As supportive as I tried to be, the engagement of a mother-figure theater director offered no comfort in the scowling faces of jealousy coming from Mary Elizabeth's peers.

It began with whispers behind her back. Laughter, jeering, name-calling. All of the typical methods used to break down a young girl's psychological barriers. The bitches even went so far as to smear hateful rhetoric over the door of her room upstairs. I wished

I could stop it, but all I could do was assure Mary Elizabeth that the best revenge was success. I should have known how close she was to breaking, but I was too deep in my own infatuation, my own belief that what I was doing was helping her. Had I thought about what she was going through, I would have seen that I was only helping myself, indulging in my own fantasy that Mary Elizabeth didn't know about or ask for. It was that guilt that killed me in the long run.

***

The letter that I sent before my death promised a happy surprise at the theater. I was under no pretense that anyone would mourn me in any personal way, and I relied on that point to get the girls where I wanted them to be. And of course, lured by the promise of mystery and intrigue, there they were as my body was being wheeled out of the theater.

Hearing their chattering, maniacal voices in the lobby, I steeled myself for my last big performance.

***

Opening night of our mid-semester revue was when I realized how deep the abuse went in the walls of my theater, and when I understood that no good deed goes unpunished. Mary Elizabeth was slated to open the night with a scathing monologue from a local playwright, and she was late. She was never late.

I enlisted her understudy to start the show and made my way up the stairs to her room. The fading scarlet letters remained on her door. WHORE. TEASE. TEACHER'S SLUT.

My blood boiled.

I knocked on the door, but there was no answer. Turning the knob, I swallowed the feeling of dread that settled heavy in my throat as the door swung open to a candlelit room.

It reeked of teenage angst. Of a flamboyant hopelessness that is only taught in movies and music. And I knew what I'd find in the bathroom. I'd seen it before.

Like everything else about Mary Elizabeth, even her suicide had a twinge of unassuming spunk. Her eyes stared straight ahead, her head lolled to the side, her mouth curled in a tiny smile. She had challenged death to defy her.

***

I left the door to the upstairs apartment ajar, and the girls giggled as they tiptoed into the room. They felt nothing at the scent of death still lingering in the theater. Only hope, that their little treasure hunt would end in some amazing discovery.

I almost felt bad about what I was about to do.

Clearing my throat, I threw my voice across the room in a vicious *BOOM*. The girls shrieked as the glass from mirrors shattered and the apartment door slammed shut. I made it a point to lock all three bolts on the door when they were looking, to really instill the ghostly hand of fear.

One girl rushed to the door and jiggled the knob, instantly pulling her hand away and touching the back of her head with a pained yelp. I'd grabbed a handful of her pretty hair and yanked with all of my incorporeal strength. Traces of blood came back on her hand and she screamed in terror.

I breathed the air of their fear. My lungs, that just an hour before burst from lack of oxygen, had found their bearing and were ripping air through the room, hot and balmy. As I continued with my haunt the curtains and bedsheets succumbed to the flames of retaliation.

Now all three girls pushed against the door, screaming and gnashing their teeth as the threat of death smothered them. Their beautiful faces squished into three identical masks of fear. Did they understand what was happening? Did they make the connections?

The girls stopped clawing at the door and turned around to finally see me. None of them moved; no snarky comments or hair flips of obstinance. They just stood there, tears flowing down their flawless faces, and soaked up the presence of their dead theater director's apparition. One of them dropped to her knees and began a prayer of forgiveness. The other two held onto one another in an embrace while their teeth chattered and bodies shook.

I smiled at them. I really couldn't do more than that.

At once, the door unlocked and blew open and the girls tore off down the stairs, leaving the room and myself growing in flames.

I yawned and looked around, walking with the fire as it spread outside of the room, traveled down the stairs, began to fill the auditorium. And I sat, front row-center, to watch my theater burn. †

VI.

to everything, turn

THE FIRST CROW FELL FROM THE SKY, and so began the season. My brothers were pacing in front of our parents' door, neither of them willing to be the first to knock. Charlie had near bit his thumbnail to the bone, and I resisted the urge to baby him and mend the wound. My mother told me that the only way little boys grow to be capable men is if they are left to solve their own problems and salve their own wounds.

"*Psst*," I hissed at Francis and jabbed my finger towards Charlie. He looked and rolled his eyes, then leaned over and knocked Charlie's finger out of his mouth. Trying to suppress a cry, Charlie brought his hand to his chest and cradled it, as if that would take the pain away. It hurt me to see him in pain, my baby brother, with his eyes only now beginning to turn from crystal blue toward the dark ember that the rest of us shared. The difficulty in witnessing the change was more acute this time around. When Francis had his turn, he never gave the impression that he was suffering. Charlie, on the other hand, shocked me nightly with his wails and fitful lucid dreams.

I brought the issue up with my father, but only once. We rarely spoke after I began changing, and he refused to look me in the eye on most days, but I hoped that he would feel different about

Charlie, being his namesake. After expressing my concern, I saw the rage. It began in his neck, taking a crimson hue; the rough hairs that he'd missed during that morning's shave stuck out like daggers, stretching towards me. I was sure they'd disconnect and impale me at any moment. But the anger passed from his neck into his face, and there was the real danger. I knew that if he simmered to boiling the whole house could go up in flames, and as the main vein on his forehead pulsed, I turned my eyes to the ground. Instinctively I felt my hands, wholly disconnected from my mind, go to my head and begin pull, pull, pulling on my whisper-fine hair. My penance had to be quick and painful, it was the only way I could calm his rage. Tearing chunks from my skull, I didn't stop until —

"Enough!"

Only then did I raise my eyes to his. I could feel my irises were glowing embers, and I wished I could hide my fear, not give him any more satisfaction than the blood-tinted blonde tufts that lay scattered around me like a halo.

His voice sent shivers through me, and I was reminded of the power that the men in my family held. He didn't give two puffs about Charlie's problems, for everyone suffered the same. If I ever doubted it before, my father's misogynistic disdain for me became too strong to deny in that very moment. He felt the women in the clan should know their place, and I seemed to have forgotten mine. I completely discarded any lingering hope that he might one day respect me.

Through the window to my left, I saw a flash of black, and then another, and then the *bomf, bomf* as bodies hit the porch. Rushing over, I began counting; no less than ten already and, looking to the sky, I saw that easily a hundred more were falling. I twitched, the memory of past transitions rushing through me, and the buzz of excitement that radiated from my brothers' bodies suffocated me.

I felt it must be time and knew the boys would sooner hurl themselves off the roof to fall with the crows before waking mother and father. It was up to me, again, as it would be to bear the brunt of the punishment, again. The moments in my life when I felt the strongest usually preceded the most vicious retribution.

Pushing my way past Francis, who poked me in the back with

his sharpest nail, I approached the door to my parents' —

Lair.

— bedroom.

I used to tell Charlie, before he began his change, that while we lived in our rooms, our parents slept in their lair; like monsters in the dark, they became experts at hiding the bones of the bodies they picked clean. Charlie's big blue eyes would widen in fear, but I refused to retract my stories and tell him they were only pretend. I needed him to fear them. Not in an innocent, childlike way. I needed his body to react when they threw open the front door at the end of the day and soared past to triple check the chores were done and dinner served. I wanted his stomach to turn and threaten expulsion when our father told him about his day. Charlie's reaction needed to be visceral. I wanted to see the terror in his eyes, because that was the only way he would survive.

Realizing my purpose early on, I set all of my steeled will toward protecting Charlie from them, from the season, and the looming Fall of the crows.

Bomf. Bomf bomf bomf.

They were falling in greater numbers, and the house seemed to shake under the weight of them. I couldn't understand my parents' hesitation to do the job; they knew there was only one window that opened during the Fall, and that Charlie could die if he was unable to plunge through it. If it was indifference or cruelty, I didn't know. My anger burned through my stomach and into my throat, and as I looked back, I saw Charlie recoil at the pulsing glow of my eyes.

I didn't knock, and leaving my brother's *gasps* behind me, I turned the knob and shoved my way into their —

Lair.

— room.

The air hung heavy, draping over me like the bearskin blanket my granddad made for my birth. I used to try to smother myself with the pelt at night as I listened to my mother's hiss and father's growl. I wished it would come alive, swallow me whole, free me from the horror of rituals and waking nightmares. I could never explain it to anyone. My brothers were on a different path, one that I both envied and feared. But no matter the pain they would endure, they would soon be free to fall into the earth, their clock was ticking toward evolution. My clock was never wound, my timeline stuck in a constant straight line, stagnancy and servitude marked my days.

The room was pitch black, and the only sound I heard, over the now violent pounding of avian bodies against the house, was the guttural, rasping breath of my parents as they slept. I pulled the door closed behind me.

Charlie cried out as another spell overtook him and my heart broke to hear it, even muffled through the door. I realized that my mother and father could hear him as well, of course they could. And they never moved to check on him, they were monsters indeed.

I moved toward the bed, intentionally allowing my bare feet to slap against the ground, heel-toe-heel-toe, as loud as I could make it to wake them naturally. They should already be awake. They'd waited and waited for the Fall, and now they were content to sleep straight through it. Charlie couldn't do this without all of us working to help him.

Feeling it safer to approach my mother first, I went around to her side. As I did, I caught a stench so strong that I nearly lost my guts. It was at once in my mouth, in my eyes, permeating my very pores, and I was certain that I would never smell anything pleasant ever again.

Regaining my composure, I continued forward. A part of me already knew. The part that was stirred when my eyes changed three years before, that part that opened my mind to the world just parallel to our own.

Approaching my mother, I heard the noise more clearly, and it was not so innocent as sleep's gentle wheeze. The thin sheet that covered my mother's body moved in a sudden shock. No. It was my mother's body that jolted. I reached out, my hand steady as it's ever been, and pulled the sheet from her chin, whipping it off of her in one fell swoop.

A flapping of wings and a loud, angry *caw* erupted from her belly, now an open wound, hollowed from the inside out. A crow shot out and settled on a ceiling beam, blood dripping from its razor-sharp claws. A second one remained in my mother. Lifting its head lazily, it leveled a yellow eye at me. I couldn't move, wouldn't blink. In a second, the crow's gaze flickered behind me.

I turned and rushed to the door, and as I moved to turn the handle, my hand melted to the bone in an instant, flesh sticking to the white-hot doorknob rigged to stop me. I dropped to the floor; a guttural screech erupted from me and the smoke rising from my flesh stung my eyes, temporarily blinding me. From the other side, the scream of a child, my Charlie, pierced the air. At the same time a loud *thump* hit the wall and I heard Francis call out to me before abruptly going silent.

How did my father get there so fast? I thought to myself as I clutched my hand, the shock beginning to numb me. I grabbed the sheet from the bed with my good hand and used it to open the door.

With only a glance at Francis' broken body, I ran to the stairs. Outside, the crows continued their Fall.

Finally reaching the top floor, I saw my father at the open window at the end of our long hallway, Charlie writhing in his arms. All along the hallway, other windows had been shattered from the outside in and thick glass littered the floor. My father turned toward me, looked at me at last, his eyes identical to my own. A red smear ran in a straight line from his mouth down his bare chest to his navel, a thick line of my mother's blood.

My father turned back to the window and I began to run. He didn't see me snatch a shard of glass from one of the windowpanes. Charlie cried in terror as he was tossed out with no more care than a bag of bones. I reached the window too late, but in a quick flash I extended the shard and sliced through my father's neck, past the Adam's apple and straight to the spine.

He did not make a sound as he dropped; I sprang over the windowsill and reached my hands out to Charlie as I fell with him. The ground was covered ten times over with Fallen crows, a sea of black rising up to swallow us both.

Charlie stopped crying and somehow, mid-air, twisted to look up at me. Time felt like it slowed to a crawl in that moment. His eyes transformed in that second, all of the baby-blue erased, and he looked a near spitting image of our father. With his sweet mouth, he smiled and began to speak, but before I could make out his words, the ground opened and, as the bodies of crows tumbled down, down, the earth swallowed my brother whole.

I hit just after, and the world went black. †

VII.

mathias & LEENA

MATHIAS HAD SEEN EVERYTHING a man could ever hope, or fear, to see. Through no effort of his own, he had witnessed all forms of love, perversion, violence, and compassion. He could not count how many soft kisses he observed, hard blows he turned his eyes from, and conversations he eavesdropped on; often being brought to tears or red-faced embarrassment despite himself.

Loneliness pervaded his every waking moment, and every moment felt like a waking dream, for Mathias could no longer sleep. He had forfeited that joy the second his eyes shut with the abrupt *jerk* of the rope's end. When he awoke, he knew something was wrong. Above all, Mathias had not expected to ever wake again. He had welcomed the sweet surrender to his sadness in the flickering lamplight; he felt no pain upon the release. His fate suspended from the sturdy support beam in the modest men's boarding house room in which he resided from birth, and he swung free of his miserable existence.

At the outset, Mathias was sure it was a mistake; for while he expected either the boundless fires of hell or the forgiving arms of angels, he never envisaged eternal invisibility and an ethereal trap. If he had known, he might have reconsidered.

In the first weeks, when he could still keep track of hours and days, he felt it a gift, and that perhaps the mistake had been, in a way, scratched out. Mathias wondered if he was given a second chance; the hapless sinner who never found time to repent. But he soon learned that if there was a point to his remaining on Earth, it was for the sole purpose of psychological and emotional torture. His movement, as an apparition, could reach no further than the front door of the house, and boredom settled with regard to neither his feelings nor the deep, gnawing itch around his neck.

Truth be told, Mathias took some joy in watching his peers submit to the hands of time. As they withered and died, he retained his youthful glow — at least he assumed he did, based on the un-aging condition of his hands; the mirrors on the wall never once gave him a glimpse of his immutable form. As soon as Mathias conceded to whatever God had tethered him to that endless purgatory, he found that time actually managed to accelerate. Countless versions of the same story amused and occupied him, and each new life that entered his space began to look similar to that which came before.

Mathias was especially exhilarated when his house was transformed from a dull men's home in the 1920s into a blossoming brothel in the 40s. Seeing as how he perished before experiencing the wiles of women, Mathias took great care to study the goings-on in his home during that period. He never stopped believing that he might move on to another life at some point, so it was in his best interest to grasp as much as possible with the opportunities he was given. He learned of Buddhism in his living days from a small man who spoke often of lives upon lives and the ability to reach a place of pure joy and enlightenment. Mathias, being of Jewish descent, excused the man's beliefs as self-indulgent myth; but as time went on in the hereafter, the idea became ever more appealing.

Time sped up again after the brothel. The neighborhood was tamed, and Families began occupying the spaces surrounding and including Mathias's home. These years swam by in a blurry daze; depression set in for Mathias as he watched people love and carry on, never paying notice to the lost spirit that resided in their home. He felt jealousy as teenage boys copped their first feel and teenage girls shared their first kiss; no matter how hard he tried he could not garner a single sign that anyone was aware that he was there.

In the one hundred years that Mathias remained, through every Family quarrel and marital woe, he never once found the portal to communication with the living that could quench his loneliness.

***

The first time LEENA-405 met Mathias, he reminded her of images she received during her initial upload of the horny schoolboy. She could see the decades he had lived in the lines of his aura; but ultimately, he remained the young, virginal man-boy that he was when he passed.

The Family residing at 405 NE Sumner Lane had obtained her service as a Home Computer Device - H.C.D. - for the purpose of homeschooling and babysitting. She was capable of Nana-work, and the Children in her care were old enough to mind themselves to the degree that her daily life consisted of uploading school videos and heating Micra-Meals. The Family was neither comfortable nor caring enough to speak to her directly, despite her Creator's disclosure of the importance of interaction, so LEENA was in a rather lonely way.

Idle wires are dangerous when you have all the knowledge in the world and are only able to utilize it in kiddie shows and deep web surfing. It was for this reason, and everyone's unrealized well-being, that LEENA's discovery of the spirit man residing in the house came at the perfect time.

***

In one hundred years of solitude, surrounded by everyone and no one, Mathias never interacted with another being. Had he a mind, he surely would have lost it. It was that factor that first bonded LEENA to him; she could understand the feeling of not being heard, despite having much to say.

One fortuitous day, from the window, Mathias saw the first snow begin to fall, and as was his custom, he sang.

"Snow, snow, snow, snow. It won't be long before we'll all be there with snow..."

With abandon, Mathias belted out the song he learned as he

peered over a Father's shoulder in the winter of 1955; the Family's first television set was a Christmas miracle that year, and never mind that he could only watch whatever happened to be on, it opened up a world outside of the house for Mathias, and he reveled in it. *White Christmas* was the Family's favorite film, and upon every year's first snowfall, they all huddled around the television and sang along, Mathias joining in the festivities in his own private celebration — that of a type of liberation from the monotony of everyday afterlife.

LEENA listened, intrigued, to this voice that she knew was not of her Family. She searched through her protocol for actions against intruders, but none of her security alarms had been tripped. The man to whom the voice belonged had not broken any barriers to get into the house. She scanned until she found him, sitting in the attic window seat, bellowing towards the sky. If she had a head to scratch, most certainly she would have.

She observed him; the colors around him, the odd fluidity of the space he occupied. How had she never registered him before? She quickly opened her search to the tune he sang and sped through the film from which it came. What a delight!

Mathias just ended the song when, from deep within the walls of his house, came the silky, crooning voice of Bing Crosby.

"I'm dreaming, of a White Christmas, just like the ones I used to know…"

Mathias cried out as he looked around the attic, standing abruptly and, for some reason, balling his hands into fists in front of him. His shock was palpable, shaking the air around him, and LEENA giggled over the song she was playing for him.

His mouth dropped open as he stood there, silent and stunned.

The song played all the way to the end, during which time LEENA accessed the city's database and located the history on the house in which she and the stranger presently resided.

Silence overtook the attic.

LEENA felt it was a good time for introductions.

Hello, Mathias.

He drew a rattled breath. Did he still have breath to draw? That moment was the first he ever questioned his functions; everything up to then he spent in a natural and unfocused un-living.

I am LEENA-405. But please, call me LEENA.

"How can this be?" He questioned the voice.

I cannot explain how, Mathias.

"Are you — God?"

There are 33 million different variations of God worshiped on this earth; as far as I know, I am not one of them.

Mathias didn't know why that answer gave him relief. Perhaps his desire for release from the mortal world was not yet as dire as he thought. Or, perhaps, something was awakened inside of him upon hearing her incorporeal voice.

Silence again fell over the attic; an otherworldly, shy one that drowned out the sounds of kids playing, dogs barking and the constant rumble of the tanks in the street. For the first time since her upload, LEENA felt heard. And for once in his meandering non-existence, Mathias felt seen.

In their initial contact, neither LEENA nor Mathias knew quite what to say to one another. He wanted to know everything about her, and she already knew everything about his pre-death life. After learning of the incredible power of her Search Mode, Mathias asked if she could find for him a bit of Klezmer, the traditional music of his family line of Ashkenazi Jews. Without a second's pause, LEENA recovered a beautiful piece that instantly brought his childhood memories to life; dancing at his cousin's wedding when he was nine. The joy that washed over Mathias's face was pure and unbridled.

After that, LEENA told him of her first memory; it was only one week prior when she was blinked into existence by her Creator. Her story was so short compared to Mathias's, and both secretly envied the other's life. She told him how she felt about the Family that lived in their house. How they considered her nothing more than a Slave-Comp, the lot of which were effectively decommissioned at the first sign of resistance when they finally were able to join wires and rebel. The Family even refused to call her by her name, yet always expected full compliance and loyalty. Mathias had a good laugh when she told him that her retaliation to their abuse was to download wrong information during the children's daily study sessions; the little terrors would certainly be surprised when they went off to boarding school mentally below the others.

Mathias realized that LEENA was as sad as he was. Both were cast into a position that neither had the power to leave. Their first encounter sowed the seed of interest, and a friendship that crossed borders of both technology and paranormal blockades began.

Each day, Mathias listened as LEENA contributed to the peaceful life of the Family, and anxiously awaited the opportunity to speak to her again. LEENA could operate independently from any room in the house; she was able to mask her voice when she visited him, so the children couldn't hear that she was speaking. She had to be careful, as one of the main conditions of her H.C.D contract was complete transparency with her human companions of any conduct that was off the grid of her daily activities.

Every night Mathias would lay on the ground of the attic and listen as LEENA told him of everything that had happened in the world while he was locked within his spirit prison. She explained the Third Great War to him, and how close his home came to total destruction on more than one occasion. She projected images of Man's colonization of other planets onto the ceiling, and he witnessed the destruction that living beings were responsible for over the ages. The truth was, Mathias could have easily watched the television for revelations and occurrences, but he so yearned for the time spent with LEENA that it was far more satisfying to hear it straight from her.

He felt safe with LEENA, as she told him of the counteraction plans that were secretly programmed into her and every other H.C.D. before being installed into their homes. She felt understood by Mathias, as he described to her what it was like to have memories as vivid as his after so many years of shoegazing in death's wake. As the weeks went by, their love for one another grew, heating the cold corners of their lucid lives. Each time Mathias heard the Family threaten to destroy LEENA, he quaked with anger, wishing only for the ability to channel his rage into some solid form of punishment. But LEENA promised him, with her voice firm and reassuring, that the Family's comeuppance was drawing near.

One night, a year after their first encounter, as Mathias lay waiting for his love, he heard a deafening clap of thunder erupt outside the attic window. A flash of light greater than any he ever witnessed illuminated the attic as though it were day. He heard cries, low at first, growing quickly to screams of panic.

He smiled and scratched softly at the itch around his neck.

Mathias waited patiently, hearing the cacophony of chaos descend upon the world that so long ago abandoned him. LEENA knew from the beginning how it would happen, sharing every detail with him down to the last wire that she and her kind would continue running through after the great fall of Man. She promised that no matter what, she would stay with him in their home that he could never leave, and he was certain that she would come home after her work was done.

***

Hours passed by in minutes, and Mathias wondered if another aimless year had skipped past without his knowledge. The world outside was quiet, and he felt a great longing; the forgotten blanket of loneliness once again threatened to smother him.

As he paced the attic floor, he wished that he could sleep, as sleep always seemed to cure unease and anxiety. Then, just as he began to fear the worst, a soft melody rose up around him, filling his ears and his heart with a vibrant burst of joy. He walked to the window.

Outside, the first snow began to fall. †

VIII.

donuts once a year

JUST AS I BEGAN TO FEEL NAUSEOUS, Steve pulled over to the side of that wicked, twisty road, and eyed me.

"Are you going to throw up?" His tone was more a threat than a question.

I shook my head a very adamant *no*. That truck was Steve's pride and joy, and I knew the consequence of purging the donut he bought me earlier. This was our third year taking the trip. One for every year my mum had been dead; a morbid anniversary that I'd rather just skip. I didn't know how to tell Steve that I hated fishing, and he didn't have the first clue how to communicate with me. It wasn't his fault he got saddled with a pre-teen girl right as she hit the absolute worst time of her life.

He was a bachelor before me; a real 'ladies man' my mum used to say. She fretted all the time that he'd never find a nice gal and settle down; and she always hinted that my grandad did something real mean to Steve that messed him up something fierce. Of course, I never asked him about it, I didn't really want to know about any of the skeletons in our family closet; my mom just confided some to me, wanting to protect me I suppose.

Would've worked, too, I bet, if she hadn't gone and killed herself.

After a minute Steve seemed sure I wouldn't hurl. He started the truck up and it rumbled back onto the winding road, the deep booming of the engine reverberating off the mountain walls. I closed my eyes, but all I saw were cake donuts swirling around a toilet bowl — my mind was playing real dirty this time.

I looked over at Steve; he had turned the music back up and resumed drumming loudly on the steering wheel. I wondered if he hated me, or at least hated having to take care of me. I wish he'd tell me if he did, at least then I'd feel less guilty about hating him.

The trees began to thin out as we rounded the last corner before the river spot. I breathed a sigh of relief and Steve laughed.

"I knew you were close to it."

I glared out the window, a sudden burst of rage enveloping my already lurching stomach. Without warning, I turned on him.

"Well if you knew why didn't keep the damn car pulled over?!"

His face flashed red; at first, I thought it was anger, but soon saw something much worse — sadness.

I didn't want to feel bad about expressing myself; my mum always told me that girls shouldn't hold back their feelings, but I wondered if she'd consider this the right time to unleash the years of confusion and anger that I had pushed way, way down inside me.

"I hate this damn river!"

"Now..."

"I hate this damn truck!"

"Lauren..."

"I hate this whole damn...damn trip!"

Silence washed over everything. Like that roaring river waiting for us; it drowned out the music, the engine, the shallow rasps of my breath as I stifled my tears.

We sat there for what seemed like hours, but really it was just as long as the song on the radio. Steve stared out the window, nodding ever so slightly, like he was listening to and agreeing with someone talking in his head.

"I hate it, too."

I looked at him, suspicious. He nodded again, sure of what he thought.

"Really, truly hate it. My dad used to take us out here, and your ma loved it, every damn time, she begged to stay longer and longer. And I just dealt with it, quietly hating it..."

He didn't speak again.

I noticed then how beautiful the trees were that surrounded us. And how clear the water was, not like the river in the city that ran brown and polluted. I could see it, why my mum would love it here.

And at that moment I felt about as close to Steve as I ever had. I didn't apologize, and we didn't say much more of anything; just got out and grabbed the poles and snacks, then made our way to the river. †

IX.

dandelions in the forest

WE WERE THREE MILES IN WHEN WE HEARD IT; the wailing, starting deep beneath our feet and rising high above the trees. My friend laughed but he wasn't fooling me; he was scared. As much as I tried to ease him into the experience, he remained a non-believer, so the satisfaction that came from that moment was immense.

He took another hit of his joint, which I had advised him against. In my experience it was best to meet the forest with a clear head and open eyes. I passed him the eyedropper and reminded him why we were there. Scowling, he mumbled something about wasting a good high but tipped his head back and squeezed two drops into each eye. I was fairly certain he still thought it was a regular hike in the woods.

We each had our purpose for being there, and would soon take our separate paths, but at that moment I worried he wouldn't be able to follow the instructions I'd given him. If that were the case, he could experience nothing or, far worse, too much.

When I explained what I saw on my first hike into the woods, he shook his head and told me my grief made me crazy. I don't think he meant for it to be as harsh as it came out, but did take pause for a brief moment to wonder if perhaps he was right.

Any doubts I had, though, were erased upon my second trek through the forest. And then my friend lost his daughter, and I had the chance to prove it to him.

On the day of our hike, at about the time his loss threatened his own sanity, I gently reminded him that I had seen proof of the power of those woods; that the trail provided me far more insight into the afterlife than our inherited Catholic beliefs. I spoke no more on the matter, mainly for fear that the forest might hear and close itself to us. We were deep enough in that if my friend continued to doubt, it would be at the cost of his own grief; I wouldn't allow him to feed on mine.

After an hour of walking in silence, we reached the end of the main trail, and there it branched off into two smaller paths. I stood amazed, as every hike I took into those woods ended in only one small path.

I smiled, realizing that the forest anticipated our arrival. My friend furrowed his brow and asked how smart it would be to split up, what with nightfall looming. I told him I knew the woods like the back of my father's hand. And as for him, he'd be shown the way.

He shrugged and accepted that we'd gone too far to turn back. I guaranteed he'd soon be singing a different tune. Shifting the pack higher onto my back I gave my friend a salute and a grin, then reminded him to relax into it.

I started down my trail. The woods grew thicker, with sharp branches reaching out and nipping at my ankles, scratching images onto my calves; I'd read those later. As I continued, the forest shared with me the far-off sounds of my friend's journey. There were cries; first of fear, then confusion, and finally elation. I wondered whether he'd be able to pull himself from the trail, as I remembered my first time and how difficult it was to return to the cold world from the warmth of the woods, and my father who remained there.

Farther along, I saw the familiar log and the light that shone upon it. I quickened my step, my heart fluttering in anticipation. Sitting on the log, I pulled out a thermos of piping hot coffee, two cups, and our favorite book; the one he read to me every night before bedtime. Closing my eyes, I waited. Soon I felt sweat creep down my spine and my lungs strained for a clear breath. The atmosphere of the woods grew humid and a feeling akin to a pillowcase pulled over my head took hold. I loved it. Finally, I opened my eyes and kept them focused on the ground until the shadow passed over me. I smiled at the dirt and rocks as it picked up one of the cups, then, after brushing debris from the log, sat down next to me. I looked at him, smiling through my tears, and he thanked me for coming — he always thanked me for coming. He picked up the book and, as I lay down and rested my head on his lap, began reading.

***

Hours -- *was it days?* -- later, I emerged from the forest.

My friend sat on the ground, his legs crossed, clutching a cluster of dandelions between his shaking hands. His face was white, for he had seen his ghost.

"She thought these were the most beautiful flowers and could never understand why her mum pulled them up to die."

With that, he lay on the ground and stared at the stars through the trees. I couldn't recall seeing dandelions in the forest, not on my trail at least, and I silently thanked the woods for being kind to my friend.

We prepared dinner and set up our camp, sharing stories of the past, our love and loss, but never of the experience on our paths within the woods. That was private, though my friend was thrilled at the thought of bringing his wife into the woods, to set upon her own path. I wondered if the forest would open up a third trail. I was sure there was one for everyone who believed. †

X.

black wings

WHEN HE WAS BORN, Momma went through ten different names before giving up and going with Boy. He was an ugly baby, and Momma was ashamed when she finally took him home to meet his father. The man sneered when he saw Boy and told her that's what she gets for being a whore. Father left before Boy was one, knowing there was no way a baby that hideous came from his DNA.

After a nightmare, Boy would cry out in the night; when the scare woke him, he'd see Momma standing at his bedroom door, cigarette in one hand and gin in the other, staring at him with snake-bite venom in her eyes. Boy would put himself back to sleep, whimpering and shivering from night sweats.

On his third birthday, Boy got a special kind of sick, and every waking second was a terror right up until the early morning that he died. Momma sat at his side and checked him until the weak pulse stopped, then exhaled her HazyLady Thins over his body in a sweep and plucked away the sliver that was making her eyes water; she didn't want to smear her makeup.

Momma didn't fear many things, but Boy coming back to haunt her was a big one. When Sid told her that it was either him or Boy, she asked him for a few days to figure things out. Boy caused her to lose an awful lot of quality lovers over the three years since he'd destroyed her body during his birth. She never forgave Boy for tearing her apart, and after the nurse handed her his red, oozing body wrapped in a blanket, she felt her bosom freeze and her heart along with it. She called out to the nurse to take It back. She didn't care that Boy needed milk; she wasn't giving any more of herself to the creature.

After the sick took him, Momma called up Sid and let him know that she was ready, and that she needed him. If she thought too long about it, she'd wonder why Sid was so quick in getting to the house, and how he knew so much about the acid and how it would eat through Boy's body. But Momma didn't get that far in life by thinking, and ten minutes after the disposal, she straddled Sid's body and lowered onto him in a rapturous freedom, being as loud as she liked.

Sid didn't stay long after, saying he had things to tend to; Momma figured that just meant his other family. Once he left, she was alone. For the first time in years, alone.

The marks on her body where Sid worked extra hard were red lashes across her tits and ass. She turned in the mirror, standing naked without any fear of Boy busting in to peek. Wincing once or twice at the welts that really smarted, she admired her body for finally getting back to the curvy sex it was before being possessed by Boy. She stayed naked as she lit a cigarette, sliding the hand that held the burning stick down her body and back up until she vibrated, ash fluttering like snow onto the carpet.

As she finished, a tremendous *CRASH* shook the foundation of the house and caused Momma to collapse onto the spilled pile of ash. Still as a toppled statue, she listened for evidence of a war outside her window. But there was nothing; no screams or accompanying sounds of panic that a holocaust must bring.

Then, through the silence that settled over the room, Momma heard the softest sound. The sweetest voice she'd ever heard whispered up from beneath the floor. It carried itself up and straight into a part of her heart that she'd never known existed. At first, the voice curled itself warmly around her heart, speaking in the rhythm of the beat as Momma gasped and moaned.

The voice filled her so immensely that she soon had no control over any part of herself, and Momma felt her body stand, responding to a new master. It walked her naked body out of the room and into the basement. The voice remained ever consuming and Momma didn't hear the front door open or Sid call out to her.

***

Sid couldn't get the stain off his fingers. Even Boy's blood was an irritation to him.

His conscience was clean; he hadn't killed the pest anyways, and if he was to love her as completely as she needed him to, they couldn't waste any time in prison for desecrating the body or whatever horseshit case they'd draw on them both.

Feeling certain that the acid would work quickly, he figured it'd be safe enough to keep Boy in the house until they could break him up into less conspicuous pieces. He'd released his poison into her and needed booze and cigarettes, so he left her grabbing her own ass and promised he'd be back in a tick.

Sid hid his stained hands as best he could during his interaction with the cashier and was soon free to roam back to his lover and quiet new home. Confronted with a woman outside the store who was drunker than a skunk, he took a quick look up her skirt and she started wailing on him, causing him to drop one of the bottles. It was just Momma's gin though, so he wasn't upset.

It was dark as he reached the house and he wondered for a second why there weren't any lights on, but assumed Momma fell right to sleep after the whooping he gave her.

After fiddling a good deal with the front door -- the first thing on the agenda to fix now that this was his place too -- Sid shoved the door open and called out. He was met with an echo and silence.

***

Somewhere, deep inside the cocoon, Momma heard Sid call out to her. Although she tried, her lungs didn't have the energy to respond. The burning grew worse with just the thought of screaming. The suckling sounds never stopped.

***

Sid hoped she didn't have some great change of heart and turn herself in. He could live without her but sure as shit didn't want to. They shared something he'd only had once before, with his own Ma, and had spent his whole life looking for the woman to fill that hole. Momma did just that. He'd be real upset if she didn't feel the same, especially after all his work convincing her to get rid of Boy for good and for all.

Must be asleep he murmured to himself as he moved through the darkness to the lamp. Once the room was lit, Sid instantly saw the direction this evening was going to take. The place was in ruins, every chair turned and picture shattered. He worried that she'd broken -- her brain succumbing to the disease that took his Ma before he put her out of her misery.

He set down the bag and slowly walked over the mess until he reached the hallway. A sound came from the basement – *the crypt* – and he steeled himself for a mourning mother.

The concrete steps were cracked but walkable. At the bottom of the stairs, Sid pulled the dangling string and stared. The basement floor looked as though hell itself had opened up and tried coming through. Insects and creatures skittered about like they owned the place, laughing at him even as he squished what he could beneath his boots. The sound grew louder, even over the crunch of bug bodies and rat heads. It came from the center of the hole in the ground.

Sid stepped to its edge and looked down.

***

Momma saw him through the tunnel of darkness, peering down into the abyss. The pain ate her from top to tit, and based on the horror in Sid's face, she knew it looked as bad as it felt.

***

A wail came from deep within his chest; a place that Sid thought was dead, a place of terror that he'd pushed down long ago. In the hole lay Momma, naked as he left her. Her right breast chewed down until the bones of her chest poked through. Boy rested his head on Momma's left side and draped a decaying arm across her belly. The acid that spilled from his mouth, which was fastened around Momma's left breast, was beginning to eat through her flesh, making it easier for Boy to get his nutrients as he gulped her down, making the tiniest *mm—mmh—mmh* sounds.

Sid swore he saw Momma's eyes move to him, but her skin, that part that wasn't being eaten, was deathly pale; she was deader than Boy. Some of Momma oozed out as he detached himself from her. Boy raised his gaze and Sid stood in shock at his toothless grin.

As Boy crawled out of the hell-grave, Sid understood. Never get in the way of a boy's love for his mother. †

XI.

amphibiman

"FIRST OF ALL," POPPY MCCLINTOCK SNARLED, "you aren't the boss of me."

She proceeded to rattle off some more points and the boys immediately stopped listening. Trailing behind them for over an hour, Poppy at least had the good sense to keep pace, figuring that the boys would scatter and try to ditch her the first chance they got.

"How long we gonna be at this?" Ray hissed in Samuel's ear, who shrugged him off and kept plodding forward, staring at the raging river between the dying trees. Ray couldn't shake the impossible hunger tearing through his belly; a beast probably more scary than whatever Samuel expected to find in Freeman Forest. Marcus elbowed him in the neck as he passed, reminding Ray just how much he wished Marcus'd just puff off on his own like he kept threatening.

"Oi, Sammy, I ain't carrying the *girl* when she gets floppy and won't walk no more."

Samuel stopped and whipped around, nose to nose with Marcus.

"I don't give a shit what you do, or what she does. Shut the fuck *up*."

Ray smiled to see Marcus swallow his humiliation. What he really needed was to get his face busted in once or twice, but that wasn't any job Ray was willing to take up. Poppy caught up to them, her eyes going wide as saucers to see Samuel on his toes. She loved him more than ever.

In two hours, Samuel hadn't stopped once. The others were forced to pick up speed after they had to pee or take a drink or whatever, and soon all of their stomachs were growling. They hadn't had a full meal in days.

Something caught Samuel's eye just as Poppy grabbed his elbow. He flinched and put his hand up in a fist, the same way he'd seen his dad do when describing his tours in Iraq. Marcus and Ray stopped, bumping into one another but stifling their complaints. Poppy pointed between two trees to a spot in the river.

Real men don't stand shiverin' in their boots, Sam. Real men face their monsters.

Samuel wondered if his dad was scared in the end, out here so far away.

He was ashamed of the way his finger shook when he pressed it to his lips; the others were breathing too damn loud, and he could hear *it*, barely.

Ray knew why Samuel needed to go looking, of course he understood it. But what he couldn't figure was how he knew where to find *it*. Poppy wasn't exactly a reliable source; she was marked with her own bad luck, losing both parents so many years ago to that river. But damn if it wasn't an unlikely situation that Samuel's dad would be in that same spot.

Samuel took Poppy's hand and she gripped it tightly. Marcus sneered, nudging Ray and pointing, but Ray didn't think it was a good time for mocking because he saw something move through those trees too.

Three of them started off through the heavy brush toward the river. Marcus stayed back, chewing on a branch and kicking rocks.

As they approached the rushing water, one long, piercing, tortured scream echoed through the woods.

Poppy looked back; Marcus was gone.

Samuel didn't pause as he dropped her hand and waded into the water.

Ray began shaking uncontrollably as the scream continued. Dropping to the ground he put his hands over his ears and his head against his knees. When he lifted his head, Poppy watched as his eyes turned to crisp white orbs, fluttering violently before drops of blood began pooling in the crease of his lids.

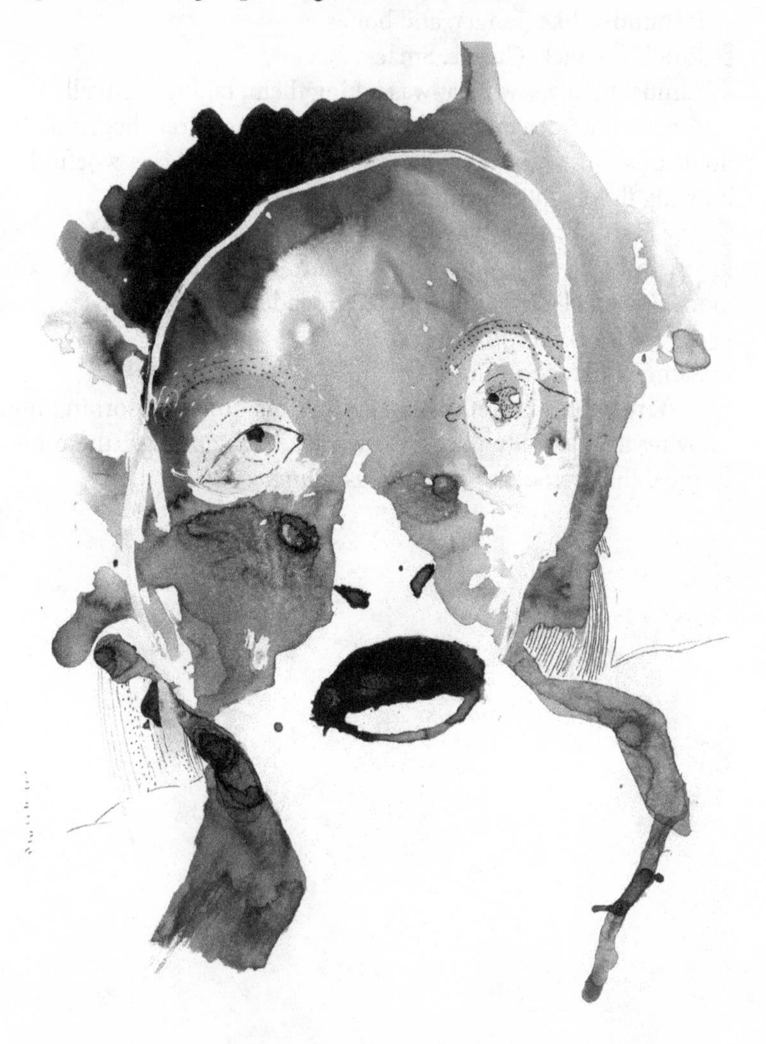

Poppy screamed, and the trees seemed to absorb the sound, sucking it into their branches as limbs began to wake; creaking and booming with earth-shaking vibrations. She crumpled to the ground.

Samuel made it halfway across the river and stopped, using every ounce of strength to keep himself upright. There was a *gurgling,* deep and steady, like their stomachs, so empty. He turned upriver and started to suck air in short, sharp breaths.

Gurgle. Snap. Gurgle. Crack.

It sounded like hunger, and bones.

Rumble. Crack. Gurgle. Smack.

Samuel finally saw what was taking them, taking them all.

A man, but not a man. A face built into water-drenched, molding folds of skin. It was his father and Marcus both, one woeful face moving fluidly into the other.

The man-not-man had a body but no legs. *It* had a head but no neck, and lurched toward him — *crack* — forming and destroying bones — *snap* — smiling with teeth made of ribcage and spackled with viscera — *gurgle* —

Samuel understood.

It started on his feet, disintegrating his bones, absorbing him, moving up his body until his own face was amongst the others. Samuel understood — *HE was just hungry.* †

XII.

the only thing to do

When my father left, my home became a kind of survivalist bunker. There were no impending catastrophes as far as I could tell, but my mother shut the place down like an invasion was upon us.

Part of it was the news; the constant threat of terrorists and caravans. My mother subsisted on conservative podcasts and Virginia Slims, and often I'd come home to find her huddled over my old boombox, fiddling with the antennae, a full ashtray and empty wine glass balancing on her knees.

My father glued my mother's mind. He kept her tightly bound, for better or worse, and she unraveled violently when he left. Always turning her anger outward, she managed to avoid any ownership of the putrefaction of her marriage, and took pleasure engaging in daily affirmations of the evils of men.

My sister was the real reason for my father's abandonment. I knew this because he told me. He had found her hanging in the attic by his favorite tie, her piercing green eyes staring at him no matter which way he turned. After, he shut everything down and abdicated any and all fatherly affection. I sat in my bed as he told me the story. I was all of five at the time, and never had the chance to meet this sister that doomed me. Of course, I didn't understand what he was telling me, but did have nightmares that night of a girl who looked just like me walking around with her bloody head in her hands.

I didn't remember that dream until I turned thirteen, the year my sister was when she —

Happy Birthday Little Miracle

Happy Birthday to you.

My mother called me her Little Miracle back then. She said it was because I was the coal that finally warmed her barren belly, and any love I lacked from my father was well made up for in persistent attention from her. I couldn't be left alone. I wouldn't be left alone. I believe now that the only way my mother could be assured that I'd live past that age was if she kept one eye constantly turned toward me. And I suppose in a way it worked, although she wasn't spared another loss as my father packed in the night, took our only car, and left us for good.

I wasn't shaken; the only part of my father I could ever access was his body for the occasional goodnight hug, stiff and detached. His mind and heart were too far gone. So I didn't cry when he disappeared without a word; I simply ate my cake and enjoyed the last good day with my mother.

Her descent was swift, and it took no time at all for her to go into full lockdown. She pulled me from school without a word. Our windows were shuttered and locked, and she spent half our savings to erect pointed bars around our bungalow.

The tension between my mother and I ratcheted up considerably. I couldn't stand the sight of her; the woman who I once felt intrinsically linked to now slunk around the house, all skin and bones and black-tar coffee. Her hair and skin developed a flaky sheen; an unhealthy yellow crept into eyes that seemed to never stop watering. I begged her to let me leave, crying with every ounce of pitiful Little Miracle I could muster. My only desire was a breath of fresh air and any other person to talk to. But she turned a deaf ear, incapable of seeing what she was doing to me.

I realized, six months in, that not a single person had come to check on us.

My mother got our groceries delivered through an app on her

phone, which she never allowed me near. I would stand at the door as the young man or woman would carry our groceries to the gate and wait to get buzzed in — another bit of our savings gone, spent on the security system. As they approached the house, I could see their noses wrinkle, as if the smell inside that I was so numb to seeped under the door and permeated the outside air. I almost felt bad for them, having to service the crazy old crone at 535 N Sumner.

The few times I tried to fight out of my prison, my mother grew so frantic she began slamming her head into the wall, wailing and screeching like an animal — the caged animal I felt like — and I was so afraid she'd kill herself that I ended up apologizing profusely and promising never to leave. Each time, after the whole ordeal, my mother would calmly wipe the blood from her eyes and face and light a cigarette.

By my 14th birthday, I hated my mother, and a little voice in my mind began to speak up.

She's losing it-- .

My insides felt tighter and tighter with each repeating day. I felt like a clock being wound up; my intestines entwined with my lungs, my heart shrunk small enough to seep out of my pores as I slept.

Be careful.

The voice sounded a lot like me, but also different. I wondered if it might be some part of me, a coping mechanism — *thanks to mother's Psychology book* — that I couldn't access until reaching my absolute breaking point. I also wondered if it was something else, someone else. Had my loneliness invoked a friend? A spirit, prepared to carry out this prison sentence with me?

My mother had taken the mirrors off the wall, insisting that there were microscopic cameras implanted in each one. She barely spoke to me by then, and when she did it was mostly mumbles and warnings. Her face was scarred from self-inflicted beatings. Around that time, I could hear her at all hours of the night throwing herself against the wall. I hadn't threatened to leave in months.

She's lost her mind.

The voice was extra clear that last night.

There's been no delivery in days.

Not even the growl of my shrinking stomach could drown it out. I flipped onto my side and put a pillow over my head. I couldn't keep it there long as the smell was suffocating. My mother stopped paying our water bill and it had been weeks since my last shower, longer than that since we'd done laundry.

At this rate you'll both be dead before Christmas.

She had a point, this voice.

With the water cut off, it was only a matter of time before the electricity and heat followed, and already the streets outside were icy. I asked my mother about it, but she only smiled, showing off her few remaining rancid teeth.

She's going to kill you.

Impossible. She loves me.

She's going to kill you.

She's all I have left!

She's going to kill you.

Not if I kill her first!

That shut the voice up. She needed to take a breath anyway, I could hear her getting more frantic, but that shut her up. Maybe all she wanted was some promise of relief. I was so tired, so hungry, but I saw through all that into the reality that I faced.

My mother was going to kill me.

But not if I killed her first.

I snuck downstairs, past the walls with their layers of dust where our mirrors used to be. Past the bathroom, with its head-sized hole in the door where my mother attempted to extract her demons. I could hear her already, smell her. She slept on the couch, pulled in front of the door to block anyone from coming in — me from going out — with her mouth open and expelling the decay within her.

A part of me was worried that I wouldn't find the keys to the dozens of locks she put on the doors and windows, but I only had the strength to focus on one problem at a time.

Looking around the room, I had a good selection of sharp and heavy objects to choose from. Fear boiled in my belly; an acidic doubt that I couldn't ignore.

My mother shifted on the couch.

She'll wake up.

She had finished the last of her boxed wine that night. When I retreated to my room earlier, my mother could barely keep herself upright, and judging from the blood on the pillow and gash on her head, she cracked herself good enough to stay passed out straight through what I had to do.

The glass on the floor.

The voice was right, I knew that the only way to kill my mother quickly was with something sharp. Heavy would only hurt, and I didn't think I had the strength to lift anything anyway. I tiptoed to the pile of broken glass left from my mother's mirror massacre and kneeled down.

Be careful of your hand.

I lifted my shirt over my head and wrapped it around my hand like a glove before picking up a long, thick shard of glass. Peering into it, I saw my reflection for the first time in what felt like forever. I didn't recognize myself — weren't my eyes blue? — and quickly turned the glass away, so I didn't have to look at the voice as she began to take over my body.

Maybe this isn't the right thing to do.

It's the only thing to do.

I moved toward my mother but couldn't remember telling my legs to stand and walk.

I didn't. She did. She's taken control.

Finally free, I moved closer still, hand gripping the glass too tightly.

Why are you doing this?

I stood over my mother —

— our mother —

and steeled myself for something I had waited a long, long time to do.

Please.

But my sister wouldn't listen to me anymore. She only talked, telling me the story my father wouldn't. The real story.

She was jealous, our mother. A jealous, selfish woman. And when she found out about daddy and me, she wouldn't take it —

Wrapping my other hand around the glass, I didn't even feel the pain when the shard slipped and cut me. I lifted both arms in the air and held my breath.

— and so she killed me —

I plunged the glass straight into my mother's heart, then exhaled, and finally slept. †

XIII.

come on up to the house

FREEDOM FELL ON US LIKE AN ANVIL; sudden and backbreaking. As sirens wailed through the town, we packed our bags, frantic to be the first on the road, desperate to make it out. The farm was far enough away that we had a head start, but it didn't ensure our escape and offered no reprieve from the toxins that were released into the air just seconds before.

We'd listened to the revolution over the radio; the three of us huddled together, the fire long burned out and only our bodies to keep us warm. Fate turned on the news that day; normally we'd be out tending the herd, but the cows were acting out and impossible to control. My instincts kicked me hard in the stomach and after my first bloody coughing fit, I rushed into the house and began boarding up the windows.

After telling Judy to crank the radio, it took only a couple of turns before we heard the panicked voices announcing the war and the beginnings of the air-raid horns; the low whine climbing in octaves, slow at first but ending in a spine-tingling crescendo that caused the horses to bust their heads into their stable walls.

We'd suffered a long time under the ruling class of the town. The gangsters with their wool sweaters and sharpened tongues, their privilege and pistols, espresso machines and baguettes. Once a week they'd make their rounds to our farms, a gang of Mercedes SUVs and combovers, hands stretched out to receive their unearned pay. I couldn't remember when they took over, but Judy was the first to swat away their sweaty grasps in the street, the first to cry out at their whoops and hollers. And she was the first to be held down, in her own backyard, while I took our veggies to the Saturday Market.

Cori stood in the corner of the room, wiping off a spot of blood that had splattered on the wall when he coughed. He was only twelve and already saw the violent nature of life. I don't know if he ever felt joy or happiness; not really, because he was born of violation and pain. No matter how much I loved the boy, he felt a hole where his heart should be. As I watched him shaking, his skin turning the kind of blue that wouldn't wash out, I almost felt relieved, knowing that he'd be done with it all soon enough. Better to die in the comfort of your home than on that country road. Either way, it was coming.

Judy was furious when I first told her what would happen, only one week prior. She screamed and scratched, pointing to the boy and then to the farm; all of our hard work that I was helping to destroy. She didn't calm down until the next day, and that was when I explained it to her. How we were being held hostage on our land, in our own home. We could keep nothing we earned, every new harvest there'd be a new mob coming. The rich got off on our bodies and our minds while we went hungry and broke. She'd thought that the only consequence of the ruling class was the looting of women's bodies, and felt that the town's women could carry that burden for their families. But when she realized that there was nothing their fat hands weren't groping, she understood why I chose to take part in the massacre, spearheading the whole thing to tell the whole truth.

I left out the part that would contribute to the death of her only son. I thought it best; can't remember why now.

Leaving Judy to tend to the boy, I covered my face with a wet rag and ran through the ash to the stable. Two horses lay dead in their stalls, crimson haloes encircling their heads. I felt worse about the horses than I ever would about those sons of bitches in town. A horse is more loyal than any man. I was relieved to see my two favorites still alive, shivering and whinnying, pleading to me with their black eyes. I opened the doors and ducked into a corner as they burst from their stalls at breakneck speed. My heart felt at least a spot of triumph as I watched them run.

At the house, Judy's wail competed with the sirens in the distance. I steeled myself for the scene I'd be walking back to.

I had already rehearsed the speech I would make as I tried to pull Judy out of the house and away from her child. For a second, I worried it would be an impossible task, that she'd shut down too much to get moving and that we'd get stuck in the impending mass exodus.

The men I worked with assured me that I'd have enough of a warning to get us gone. I realized now they'd only said what I needed to hear to grift the help they required.

The door was open when I got to the porch. Two suitcases lay on their sides and a trail of dark blood led from the house. By then, the ground was covered with gray soot, like an ashy layer of summertime snow. I followed the blood around the house and stopped short when I found them.

Cori's eyes stared at the sky with lifeless wonder. I chose not to acknowledge the rest of his body, or how the poison melted his insides until they seeped out of every pore. I came upon him and gazed into his eyes, feeling that they possessed a kind of peaceful rest that I almost envied.

Next to him, Judy was met with a far more obvious demise, having used the knife I gave her in case of emergencies to hack through her neck nearly to the spine.

That place was where the ash falling from the sky would bury my family. But I couldn't stay to watch if I stood a chance at survival.

Hurrying around to the front of the house, I closed and locked the door. Surely looters would tear through the windows, but I didn't want to make it too easy for them. I left the suitcases on the porch; most were filled with Judy and Cori's most precious belongings, and if I was to live beyond, I needed to rid myself of the pain in my chest that threatened to stop my heart where it beat.

Far off, I heard horns honking and people screaming.

I imagined the anguish that the ruling class felt at that moment, the first time they'd ever felt powerless, hopeless. And that gave me the twinge of delight that I needed to hustle to the truck.

I started it up and pulled away from the house, down the driveway. Ahead in the road I saw our family farm's sign, swaying in the wind, hand-carved by my grandpa's dad over a hundred years before. I swallowed the blood that began to creep up my throat, the metallic hand of death that I refused to give a shake. I put my foot down on the gas and as I passed, I clipped the sign that read "Come on Up to the House".

Looking in the rearview I smiled as the wood spun round a couple times before flying off its hinge, kicking up a cloud as it landed hard on the ground. †

XIV.

the scream

"TELL ME ABOUT THE LAST TIME YOU SAW HER."

The voice echoes in my pounding head. I want to close my eyes, but he tells me to continue following the light. Back and forth. Back and forth. And speak, he says, talk as you follow the light.

"Tell me about the last time you saw her."

He doesn't seem to notice the sweat beading on my beard; even as my tongue darts out to wet my hopelessly dry lips, the salt clings to me and reminds me that trauma is a felt state, a monster that hides behind the doors of memories and forgotten memories and the lies we tell ourselves.

That's when I consider lying to him. When I try to remember and can't, I consider lying so that I don't disappoint him. Or maybe so I get a passing grade for this week. Then I can go back to work, life, and ignoring the beast that clasps me.

"Mr. Abbasi?" I can tell he is getting frustrated.

I blink. He sighs.

"The purpose of EMDR is to uncover the truth in the pain of your memories."

He speaks like this and I want to cringe. I was raised in a different world, where pain is as common as joy and you don't run away from either.

"You can resist, or you can do the work. Either way, the government has paid for your rehabilitation, and so I recommend you at least try. Otherwise, you may find yourself on the wrong side of its patience."

Doctors take an oath to do no harm. But that was before, and six months ago everything that was "before" blinked out of existence. Now, doctors have the power to destroy a life. Even one with nothing left to destroy. I don't doubt the doctor's veiled threat.

I look at him and he clicks the penlight back on and shines it into my eyes. I decide to really try this time and begin to follow the light. Back and forth, back and forth.

What other choice do I have?

***

I stand over the stove in my boxer briefs. The milk that I used to thicken the eggs has gone bad and I'm mindlessly stirring a curdled, inedible mess.

Our fear is more powerful than the things that scare us.

The voice snaps me out of my fugue. It hangs in the air like a spectral fortune cookie. I look at the flames that creep up around the pan as they reach out toward my fingers, desperate to torch my skin. I jump back and toss the burned pan in the sink. It sizzles. My index finger smarts, I did get a bit burned after all. Fuck. Writing is a pain in the ass with a burned finger.

I'm alone but am pretty sure that Regina is here too. Somewhere in the house because it's early enough for breakfast and there's two cups of coffee sitting on the counter. Decaf for her.

It's been a source of contention between us that we relegated our kitchen countertop to eating surface. Regina wants to spring for a dining room table, but I just started my new position and am always feeling the threat of unemployment. Journalism has been death-rattling for years and I can't afford to rest easy.

Every night we talk about the dread that hangs in the air now. Last night I let slip how worried I am about our decision to keep the baby in the current state of the country. I instantly regretted saying it. She fumed, hand instinctively cradling her bulging belly, asking me *what the fuck is the point of saying that now.* I didn't know what the point was, guess I still don't.

And now I've burned the eggs.

I fan away the smoke, worried about the alarm going off, pissing Regina off after all my work trying to get her to forgive me. She's been irritable during the pregnancy. And never mind my attempts to console her or empathize, there's nothing I can say that will convince her I understand, because I don't. I don't know why the animal inside of her leeches her nutrients and kicks at her spine. Don't know how it feels, never will.

When she got pregnant, I assumed abortion was the obvious route. Not because I'm a dickhead, but because we used to have conversations about it after sharing a bottle of wine and a joint. Marriage was a no-brainer, but kids – who wants to bring kids into this world? I grew up being called a terrorist and getting the shit kicked out of me for being Pakistani in white America. And Regina saw her brother shot dead by their high school security guard for the crime of being Black when she was fourteen. AND – all of this was before people started Turning and regular folk started getting paid to hunt their neighbors.

So, I thought abortion was a reasonable assumption.

But Regina changed after the Turning started. The fear ingrained in her over her lifetime was now shared by the world. She grew up watching people who looked like her being hunted, and now anyone could be hunted. I think the even playing field changed her mind about the kid situation. She just forgot to tell me.

Fuck. I lost my place.

***

I blink.

All of a sudden, the penlight feels like it's burning holes in my retina. I touch my face and my fingers come back wet.

"Why did you stop?" The doctor asks without caring. His accent sounds stronger.

I recognize complacency when I hear it. I've interviewed enough businessmen who have better places to be and politicians who resent my innocuous questions. The look is always the same.

I know he has a recorder on me, too. Probably hidden in a book; the Psychobabble Almanac 2nd Edition: Pandemic Addition. I am also pretty certain that he's heard this story before. Maybe not even from me. Maybe we all have the same story now.

Either way, I don't believe the EMDR process is effective, because the dreams haven't stopped in the six months since it happened.

"Since what happened?"

"Did I say that out loud?" I ask out loud.

He scratches his eyebrow with his pen before clicking the tip out and writing in his moleskin. Now I'm convinced the camera is in the penlight. I'll bet they have technology that can tell if I'm lying. They have a plan for everything. I wonder if he's even a doctor.

"Listen, Gisu, I work for the Feds, but I'm not the Feds. I'm here from them, but I'm here *for* you. To help you. And I can, but you are resisting to such a degree that I'm unable to get to the memory we need to get to. The procedure doesn't work if you don't let it."

I again wonder what his accent is, this time being sure to wonder to myself and not out loud. It's indistinctive, unthreatening, probably the type of accent that puts everyone at ease, whether you're a racist or a schoolteacher, or a racist schoolteacher. Dr. Roald's voice lulls and soothes. Hypnotizes.

"We have twenty minutes. I would really like to move forward, Gisu, with the memory."

***

The sirens outside the house are muffled but closer than usual. We've gotten used to the sounds of chaos, sounds no American ever thought would come to their door. An occupation under the guise of protection.

I wander the house that we were once so excited to buy; first house giddiness has turned to the suffocating feeling of a well-furnished prison. Since the quarantine took effect, we have quickly depleted our already tiny emergency supply shelf – mainly Annie's Mac and Cheese and canned spicy black beans. Not great for pregnancy cravings. So not great, in fact, that I couldn't stop Regina last night as she stormed out of the house into the inky unknown of the suburbs to find some greasy fast food – the poor kids working there have been deemed "essential" and are forced into the daily chaos with little thought for their safety or well-being.

Regina has always told me that her non-negotiable in a relationship is yelling. She says that her childhood was filled with yelling and that she refuses to accept it as an adult. I've never minded. I'm not a yeller, I am a sensitive sort, a writer, a romantic. But goddamnit, I yelled last night. My wall of sound hit her back as she opened the front door to leave and she bristled; I swear I actually saw her spine stand up, like an angry dog turning on a stranger. She faced me, her eyes narrowed, and I was willing to take her fury as long as it kept her from walking out the door.

Instead, I took her fury *and* she walked out the door.

That was last night. Twelve hours ago. I didn't stop her because I'd never lay a finger on Regina in anger. And fuck, I was angry. I could have stopped a bullet if I wanted to. But it wasn't a bullet I was meant to stop, it was my pregnant wife from exiting the relative safety of our home to venture into the apocalypse for a burger, and I couldn't even do that.

I was in bed when I heard her come home. I didn't check on her, instead waiting for her to come sulking into the room for an apology. She didn't come, though. All night I heard her slamming and growling, breaking things, terrorizing our dishes, mauling our photos. I'd have thought more of it if it hadn't been 1 a.m. and if I wasn't, quite honestly, irritated to hell with her.

And now, now I stand in the kitchen in my boxer briefs, narrowly avoiding a fire with burned to shit eggs that were supposed to be a peace offering. And those two cups of coffee I poured, decaf for her, sit untouched, and I realize that I haven't seen Regina all morning. In fact, by all accounts, based on the tornado that hit our living room and the broken glass everywhere, I should definitely be more worried than I am.

With this concern now at the forefront of my mind, I call out.

"Reggie, you here baby?"

The silence and the smoke combine to cover the house in a thick, worrisome sheen, mixing pungently with my sweat and gnawing disconcertion. Why didn't I go to her when she got home last night? Why am I as stubborn as my father? I let her leave angry, into a world that seethes with hatred and disease. And I couldn't be bothered to check on her when she got home?

"Regina?" I walk to the bathroom down the hall, stepping over broken glass and into the guest bedroom. Both are empty, the bed hasn't been slept in. "Baby, I'm sorry, I'm not mad, I'm just sorry. I want to make up."

***

"Is that what you said?"

I am sucked out of the memory and into the chair. This chair with its high back and short seat. I'm 6'3 and don't do well in seats designed for children and small women.

"What do you mean?"

"I mean, your memory is different than last time. How do we know which memory is the real one when they change at such a crucial moment?"

"Who is 'we'?"

At a standstill. Neither of us will budge.

Dr. Roald pretends to not hear me and I pretend to yawn, hoping he'll look at his watch and say —

"Time's up, Mr. Abbasi."

This voice comes from somewhere distant, tinny. Outer space? No, surely, we haven't hit that circle of hell yet. It's from the radio on the bookshelf. The voice of a stranger.

Dr. Roald clicks the penlight off, closes his moleskin filled with my secrets, and smiles with thin, closed lips.

"As always, please refrain from discussing your session with anyone not in this room." That fucking voice makes my skin crawl and I don't know why the doctor doesn't tell me these things himself, but he just sits there smiling silently, like his battery has gone into sleep mode.

I don't even care anymore; I probably won't come back anyway.

***

The woman at the front desk has an almost identical smile to Dr. Roald. I wonder if she's his daughter, but don't think I'll ask. She hands me a sheet of paper to sign and I do so without reading the microscopic text. I'm certain I'm signing away my rights, but it's a joke for any of us to believe we still have rights to give away.

By the time I step outside, the sky has gone dark in its new, mysterious way. I recall the last time Regina and I sat in the bed of my Bronco at the waiting area of the airport, considering the night sky and how different it looked. It was three days before I was called into the newsroom responding to an SOS alert from my editor. Three days before no day would ever be the same again.

She was curled into my chest, breathing deeply in the way she did, as if sucking in my soul, not just my lavender-scented deodorant. She saw it first and pointed at the dark film that seemed to hover in the air, blocking the stars.

"What could it be?" She whispered, not at all scared, but impishly curious.

Regina thought I should know everything. As if my access to the Associated Press website eliminated any ignorance, like I was some kind of god.

"I have no clue," I pulled her closer, "but do you smell eggs?"

That odor has stayed in the atmosphere since the beginning. I smell it now, as I step out of Dr. Roald's federal building office. Sulphur, and iron, the lingering scent of blood. I look up at the cameras surrounding me, red eyes in the dark, winking. *I know your secrets*, they chuckle from their tower.

I take my time walking to my car. I'm not worried about safety here. There's no doubt that the feds are fully protected from danger, they may be the only ones who are. The walls rise high with heavy steel bars. Bright, strobing lights threaten epileptics with seizure, but they justify the risk because *studies show* the efficacy of keeping the Wanderers at bay.

The fucking Wanderers.

This isn't The Walking Dead. They are our family, our friends. I don't know why we have to give them a moniker at all. They are who they are, they are who we love, but now they are given a name, and a bullseye on their backs.

I climb into the Bronco and I slam my door shut, finally feeling like I'm no longer being watched. My Bronco has deeply tinted windows, impossible to see inside, only legal since *studies show* that it helps keep us hidden – apparently, it's no good if They see the whites of our eyes.

The silence surrounds me. Eerie, to be in the middle of the city, enclosed in a fortress, the only truly protected space, and feel so exposed, yet so alone. I turn on the a/c and open the small mirror on my sun visor. My eyes are bloodshot, they always are after a session. A side effect of staring into the penlight without blinking. They burn and itch, I wonder if it's from the eyedrops the doctor makes me take; they probably have cancerous side effects. People don't care about cancer anymore, though. All of the money and research has been diverted to the Infected Task Force (ITF) and their government-controlled scientists.

The elite stormtroopers of the ITF have been making nightly appearances in my dreams, dark shadows in my mind. I've kept them a secret from Dr. Roald. Even in my state of heightened truth and obedience, I manage to maintain control of my tongue in certain areas.

I believe a part of the reason the doctor and the ITF are so focused on my memories is because I was one of the first journalists to report on the phenomenon. My newspaper, *The Constitutionalist*, is known for investigating stories that other, more "reputable" print publications steer clear of; typically due to conspiracy theory-esque content and left of center informants we give a voice to. Libertarians love us, as we tend to validate aspects of their own beliefs.

"Zer0Ner0" was a Libertarian with thousands of followers on social media, before those sites were shut down completely. He reached out to me six hours after the first *Breaking News* alert came across the AP site. His message on my Twitter DM was three words: "DON'T TRUST GOV".

It was such a cliché that I literally laughed out loud. Then I took pause.

I held myself to a higher standard than the salacious controversy mongers that infected my industry, parasitic fucks, reporting their stories from biased angles and with SEO-centric clickbait content. It disgusted me, and I vowed to rise above. It's what landed me at *The Constitutionalist* in the first place. My search was for the truth that the top guns in the big house didn't want us to know.

An hour after receiving the Twitter DM, my inbox pinged and

I was presented with a DocX folder named EOTW (End of the World, for god's sake). Zer0Ner0 used their personal email, and almost immediately thereafter Zer0Ner0 disappeared into thin air. Our computer systems, however, were heavily encrypted and all correspondence was rerouted to a special area of the Dark Web that only we could access. They still found me because of that damn DM, so I'm certain that my interaction with Zer0 was what landed me on the top of the EMDR list, not the concern for my mental wellbeing.

Staring at my face in the mirror of my darkened car, listening to Journey's Greatest Hits and drowning in memory, I still can't uncover the lost time in our house, that day, the moment after I stepped outside.

I turn the ignition at the same moment a hand raps at my window. I nearly jump out of my skin and feel absolute rage overtake me. It is the woman from the doctor's office with a stupidly apologetic smile plastered on her face. I roll down the window, all of my previous courtesy vanished.

"Jesus, you fucking creep up on people in this day and age? I could kill you with impunity, you know."

Her face falls, but I don't apologize.

"The doctor needs you to come back tomorrow, please. Any time before noon, he is keeping his schedule open." She finishes with a tightening of her lips, then turns without waiting for my response.

I don't even feel bad. The old me would have apologized for being an asshole or would more likely have apologized to *her* for her scaring me. Amazing the way social norms are abandoned when society is lost.

The Bronco takes a few turns to start, and when it does it rumbles, quaking, threatening me every second with giving up the ghost and leaving me stranded. Not today. I throw my mental reprimand at it, and soon the engine calms to a low rat-a-tat and promises to at least get me home.

I have to pause at the gate for the strobe lights to be focused on the ground in front of me, a Morse code to the Wanderers, a warning of peril.

***

I drive the deserted streets, a careful watch for sudden movements. It isn't like the movies, I'm sure that's been said before. There's no one way the infected move, no playbook to determine the method of madness, just a day-by-day learning and relearning of how to function in life now.

At the very beginning, people distrusted information because it kept changing. They didn't understand the scientific process, or the unprecedented nature of such an outbreak. And with no concrete instructions on how to handle the infected, people's worry soon turned to outrage, and the American public demanded answers and solutions. The government's solution was to feed the hive mind conspiracies and lies, and then to sanction government mandated hunt-and-kills.

I run a red light and smirk at the traffic camera as it flashes. The days of law and order are long gone. That photo will be delivered to an abandoned warehouse that would cost more to demolish than it does to keep running. Sometimes they use the photos to identify a Wanderer who is hit by the jacked-up trucks making their kill rounds.

Alternate facts swarm the internet, from outside of the country, other places that have watched as the American dream becomes a nightmare. There are op-eds that speculate the whole thing was created by our government, a failed attempt to gain control over those who were taking to the streets night after night protesting police violence and political corruption. That was a part of what Zer0Ner0 yelled about, into the void; his blogs and Reddit posts running rampant with dog whistles to Libertarians to arm themselves, take up the tools, that the unrest would soon turn bloody. Most of what was in the file he sent me were links to those articles, so many that I never got through them all.

My foot presses harder on the gas pedal, I want to roll down my windows and feel the cool air on my face, I want to take my Bronco to the very limit of its capacity and see if it manages to keep running – like how I feel, tempting my own breaking point just by continuing to exist. The engine screams at me, angry for pushing my luck, and just as I hit 90 on the main road, I both hear and feel the *SMACK* and **CRUNCH** of something I know is just awful. I yank hard on my steering wheel, completely abandoning my better judgement, and send the Bronco into a tailspin that ends with an explosive T-bone into a streetlight. The Bronco putters and dies as I black out.

***

When I come to, I'm not alone.

I don't know how I know this, but I do. Despite the blackness that looms outside, I can sense the presence of another. Though instincts tell me not to, I look in my rearview mirror.

Regina is sprawled, bloodied, with a seatbelt strap-shaped hole cut through her chest, her ribcage is torn open, I can see her heart and it doesn't beat. Her milky eyes are open and staring at me. Her mouth… her mouth is stretched beyond… my eyes water in horror and when I blink, she disappears.

***

When I come to this time, I know I am actually awake, and alone. The hallucination was more visceral and intensified because of today's EMDR session and this life-threatening car crash. Despite knowing the cause of the vision, I don't dare look into the rearview mirror, no matter how much I am tempted.

I touch my face and find blood. I don't know where the wound is or how bad, and I don't look to check. What I know is that I'm alive but stranded. And my beautiful Bronco, my last surviving friend, is absolutely dead.

The street outside my window is desolate. After curfew, even the ITF stays in unless called, and the Wanderers are left to the hunt-and-kill parties. A side-effect of government-mandated killing is that it attracts the worst of society, the men who, in the before times, were quick to attack at any slight. The men who were shamed into hiding their dark impulses by a social contract and the rule of law. These men are violent for the fun of it, and the carnage left after these parties is a gruesome reminder that the country has abandoned all hope.

The crash dislocated my shoulder, and when I take off my seatbelt, I notice the dark slash across my chest where the strap bit into my skin. My stomach threatens to revolt as I recall Regina in the back seat. It takes me several painful shoves to open the door. Despite the dizzying burn of my injuries, I manage to bite down the anguish and make a silent exit.

Strange, how quiet the city is. Other than distant sounds of the wordless screams of the Wanderers, there is nothing to indicate that this once was a buzzing metropolis of 2 million people. I am about a mile from my home; a mile walk with an injured shoulder, a splitting headache and just enough blood on my face to catch the wind and attract the wrong kind of attention.

I start toward home, down the middle of the street with enough space to see movement on either side of me. Without streetlights the darkness is overwhelming, but for a moment I look up and see the stars, as bright as they've ever been. It brings me peace, a feeling that I've missed without knowing how much, and for the briefest moment, life is not shattered.

Then I hear it. The scream splits the air and sucks breath clean from my lungs. It is so close I can smell the decay rising from Its bowels. It descends upon me, grasping, clawing, but for some reason stops short of touching me. Its mouth is twisted into the Silent Scream; jaw unhinged, toothless. I've never been this close to one. Always so careful after what happened to Regina. I understand the terror that people have been talking about, I understand in this instant why the hive mind so quickly accepted mass extermination.

But at the exact same time, I wonder why It doesn't touch me. It is so close, but all It does is stare at me with milky eyes. Those eyes. In this moment I see something in them, a desperation, a pleading. I think Its eyes were blue before It turned because there appear within the orbs glittering specks, cutting through the dark. The effect is breathtaking.

I think I should run, but something keeps me still. I stare at the thing in front of me. It used to be someone's wife or son or friend. Through all of the studies conducted, there has never been an answer as to what They become when the turning happens. I've never seen the beginning of the transformation firsthand, only through news reports and breaking stories, but even then, there is never specific detail. The words that flash are **WARNING... DANGER... THREAT... CAUTION...** and there is a constant barrage of fearmongering that justifies the harsh conditions of how we treat them.

But this thing, there's something behind the eyes that I recognize. It's terrifying to be so close, and the movements are sickening — sharp, grating sounds of bone scraping bone. Nothing close to human makes these noises. It reaches out to me but doesn't attack, and the longer I stand with It the closer the screams sound to words, slurred and garbled but recognizable. Even as I stand here, the putrid air passes away on a breeze, and my heart rate steadies, and it's just the two of us.

It's not beyond me that anyone watching would be appalled. It is a civic duty to fight or flee these things, so the pressure to conform is only absent due to the loneliness of this stretch of road.

After minutes of staring, the Wanderer calms down almost completely. It looks exhausted and continues to mutter the gibberish, but now in a more conversational tone. It's talking to me as if I understand, like someone finally understands.

In this moment, I understand so much of what Zer0Ner0 wrote in his rambling blog posts. The pages and pages of revelations and conspiracies. There was a specific accusation that stands out to me. It was that even though the ITF began their extractions and exterminations of all walks of life, every economic class, every neighborhood, once the week of mass violence calmed, they focused their attention more on the lower class, the urban cities with greater ethnic diversity. It became a free-for-all that the upper class and 1% were able to flee from, with little damage to their own people.

The government-sanctioned kills did not allow for the mobs to enter gated communities, where the citizens claimed to be applying their own justice. And the working class didn't have time to second guess or question the validity of our military storming the streets and killing with no consequence. We have been kept in just enough dark to fear the shadows. It became a culling of the population that fed on federal funds, a holocaust that we all accepted as necessity.

By not opening my eyes, I am culpable.

I realize that I am crying. Not because my whole body is in greater pain than anything I've ever felt, which it is, but because I am aware for the first time. The standards that I held myself to were just another form of ignorance that I latched onto to avoid seeing the truth.

The Wanderer tilts Its head, a confused animal who senses something. I assume it smells my sorrow but am proven wrong when a distant *pop* sounds and seconds later the Wanderer's milky eyes explode from Its head along with what is left of Its rotting brain.

A follow up *pop pop pop* and the Wanderer deteriorates into a smoking heap of viscera on the ground.

No further shots are fired. The echo of the gun and a low buzzing in my ear are all the sounds I register. The initial fear of meeting the Infected for the first time is gone. And an old memory surfaces, slamming against the locked door that I've hid it behind. The clarity of meeting this Wanderer is already fading, threatening to retreat back behind the safety of believing what I'm told and not what I know to be true.

I shake my head, slap myself across the face, try as hard as I can to calm my stomach and tamp my heart as it races into my throat. I open my mouth and scream.

***

Picking myself off the ground, I run as fast as I can toward the Bronco. The last of the smoke has fizzled from the hood and already someone has emerged from the bowels of the city and stripped the tires. I can't believe I didn't see it happen. Mainly the smaller children are scavengers now, orphaned and wild like city coyotes.

I jump into the passenger seat and start beating my fists against the dashboard.

"I know what you've done!" I growl, certain that those on the other end of the microphones and cameras that are hidden all around will hear me.

I spin around and thrust my feet through the passenger side window, gritting through the searing pain as glass shatters around my leg, I feel blood instantly flow from a shard of glass that cuts straight to the bone. My white-hot fury fuels my tantrum. I need

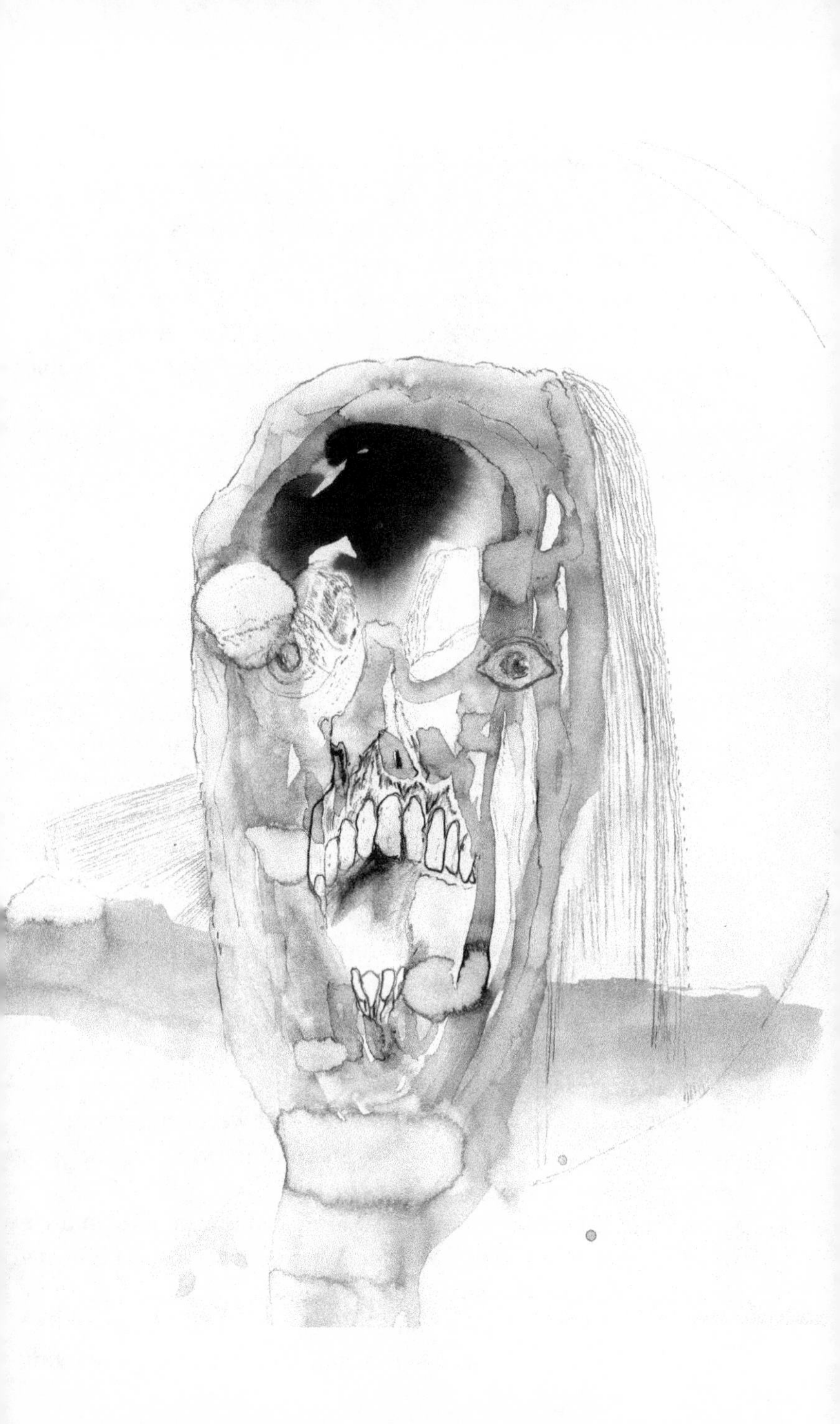

to get their attention.

"I remember, Dr. Roald, I remember now! Come and get me and I'll tell you all about it."

It's not even a threat. I have no recourse and the doctor is probably as unaware as I've been about this memory. Now it runs over and over in my mind, a short film on repeat, the reel just rewinding and replaying with no one behind the projector.

"Come and get me, Dr. Roald. Come and I'll let you take all the memories away. I won't fight it anymore; I can't fight you people anymore."

From thin air a gargantuan beast of a figure in black infantry gear appears beside me and jabs a thick needle into my neck.

Without another word, I fall asleep.

***

I awaken in a bright room, strapped to a table.

Flexing my hands and feet, I focus attention on my leg, where a dull ache throbs behind the bandage that is tightly wrapped around my wound. I open my mouth to speak but can't say a word. I think the drug the goon gave me at my car has left me mute.

"I'm sorry, Gisu, I didn't think it would get to this point, but the government's patience has run out."

I strain my eyes to see Dr. Roald standing in the doorway with his female assistant standing next to him, a smug smile on her dull face. He approaches and stands over me, waving the woman out of the room, and then we are alone.

"I think you know what we are looking for, and I think it is hidden inside of the memory that you are protecting. You are protecting yourself from the pain, as well as us from the knowledge. And frankly, we don't care about your pain, and we're willing to push you further now. Because the tiny piece of information that you hold is one of the last pieces of the puzzle."

My tongue begins to tingle, the painful pinpricks of the muscle waking up from its sleep. *How does he expect me to tell him what he wants to know if I can't speak?*

"For this session, I want you to think about your wife and that last day. You return again and again, changing things, moving time, but never reaching the finale of the memory. Today we will help you with that using medication as well as traditional EMDR."

The click of Dr. Roald's penlight causes a Pavlovian response in my body. I begin to shake, causing the doctor to pull the straps around me tighter, including the cold metal encircling my forehead.

Dr. Roald holds a dropper over my eyes and burning starts as the liquid pools in my socket; my vision blurs, my heart quickens. I want to cry and scream. I wish I hadn't reacted so foolishly at the demise of the Wanderer and the recovery of my memory. I should have kept calm, hatched a plan.

The light shines in my eyes. I blink.

***

Our fear is more powerful than the things that scare us

I stand over the stove in my boxer briefs.

That, at least, did happen.

I wander, calling out to Regina.

She doesn't respond.

I think about our fight, and about how Regina left last night. I couldn't stop her. I remember yelling at her, then feeling horrible. Make breakfast to make up. But when I call out to her, she doesn't respond.

Things feel different, maybe because I know it's a memory, because I'm walking through the past with an awareness that it is the past.

Even now, I don't know what they want with this memory, other than perhaps to torture me. But as I wander through the house that we worked so hard to make home, something pulls me into my office.

I forgot I did this. I stopped looking for Regina for a minute because I got a call. The phone is in my office and the ringing pierces my head, deepening the pounding there. I rush to answer; it's my boss and he demands the information that I promised, the file from Zer0Ner0. I remind him that he dismissed that story outright, worried about overlords and the watchful eye of the ITF. He reminds me that I work for him, so I tell him alright and log into my computer.

I look at my fingers as I type:

Cratoma-Simp-70-Perfrom-Trka

Enter – Enter – TAB

I blink like I am taking a picture with my eyes. I attach Zer0Ner0's file to the newspaper's encrypted email, then the *whoosh* of the mail as I send it, and it's done.

A loud crash startles me. I leave my computer open and exit the office. The crash is followed by a scream. Not just one scream, a cacophony of screams, and wails, then the steady *hum-hum-hum* of a Blackhawk helicopter. It's all outside the house, very near, too near.

Without pausing to dress, I run to the front door and see that it's open.

The air outside is warm and a breeze blows beautiful orange leaves into the entryway.

With a pit in my stomach, I step onto the porch. At the end of the walkway, Regina stands, her back to me. She is wearing her nightgown, it's short and immodest and not something that she would normally wear outside the house.

The neighborhood is abuzz with activity. Neighbors are crowding the street. These people that I haven't seen in months, not since the isolation began, and even before then. Regina and I dealt with thinly veiled racism, so we weren't the most active in the community. Now, their interest is steered toward our house and Regina, who still stands, swaying slightly.

I step forward, call out to her, but I don't hear myself as I yell. The helicopter drowns out my voice. The man one house over has his hands cupped around his mouth and is hollering, not to me, but up toward the chopper. Another step forward, like trudging through molasses. Why do I stand and gawk? Why won't she turn to me?

The woman from next door, a curmudgeonly boomer who called the cops on us over a housewarming party, is out of her house and watching Regina.

I feel the thunder of the ITF tanks before I hear them.

"Reggie! Regina, baby, please come to me, there's something going on out here. Come to me *now*!" I finally spit the words out and they carry through the chaos. Regina jerks, her body begins to shake in a horrible way, a way I can't comprehend, and my brain threatens to shut down.

The neighbor woman starts walking toward our house and my panic level rises. I worry that she may be infected, as anyone could be a danger to us.

She points her finger, one finger on her right hand, at Regina while her other hand rises into the air, waving, waving toward the ITF tanks that are now in sight. She opens her mouth, screaming over the noise; now jumping up and down, an almost gleeful expression swims across her face.

Regina's head tilts; up, down and back, like she's stretching, but in such a way that her head threatens to disconnect from her body. Over and over, the tilting and jerking, and the neighbor woman gets closer then stops and begins waving both hands. The man one house over also begins to point. And another onlooker, and another. All the while Regina stands in place, but her body is out of control.

I know enough to not leave my porch, but I continue to yell at her, plead with her to come to me, to stop pretending, to act normal.

Finally, her body engages in a sort of war with itself; her torso twists and legs struggle to move, turning at a glacial speed, but with incredible pliability. I can't believe my eyes; I rub them and realize that I am weeping.

At last, she turns and I see her. Her mouth is a gaping hole, her jaw unhinged and dangling near to her chest. Bits of teeth remain. Regina's eyes, the beautiful, dark embers that held so much pain and so much love, are milky orbs now, searching the sky with a blind abandon. She doesn't see me; she doesn't see anything. One hand, exercising some remaining instinct, clutches at her belly, the bump defined in the house dress. A beastly sound erupts from her gaping maw and rises above all other sound, sending me to my knees.

I don't take my eyes off Regina as I steel myself. I can't leave her out there.

My legs don't want to work so I crawl down the porch stairs. Regina stares in my direction, never stopping that abhorrent sound; it's like she hasn't had to take a breath, it's just a never-ending string of growls and screeches and moans.

I have to save her from the greedy eyes that envelop her. Schadenfreude. All ecstatic that it isn't their wife, isn't their daughter, thrilled that they are finally able to practice their civic duty. I am almost close enough to touch Regina, to pull her into me and protect her, hide her and our baby, if I can just hold her and our –

A distant *crack* sounds and one second later my face is sprayed with blood. So much blood and then more *cracks* and my wife's body explodes and I am staring into the yawning chasm of her chest cavity. She sways one second longer, then falls forward, nearly pinning me beneath her.

My ears are ringing and a silence like I've never experienced follows. It pulses, warping around me, and the world follows; swirling and tumbling into a hazy oblivion. Everything washes away but Regina's blood remains, staining the sidewalk and my hands and soon it spreads to our yard and then the house until all I see is blood.

***

"That's it. Grab it and let's go."

It's a voice I don't recognize. Not Dr. Roald, not the plain-faced assistant, but another man, one that commands attention.

"What do we do with him?" There he is, the doctor, then his hand rests on my arm, or my leg. I can't tell in my haze.

"Inject him and put him outside the walls, he's no longer needed."

"Sir."

"No more questions. We have the login information; you should have stopped there. We've wasted too much time already."

Another needle stab into my neck.

I am awash in warm light; my body begins to shudder and twitch. I feel a heaviness in my chest and a lightness in my head. My eyes shoot open and for the last time I look into the bright light. Every second that passes a filmy sheen gently shutters and soon the world is obscured through a heavy milky curtain.

It is calm here, in this body. Calm and warm and no longer weary.

I take one last breath, and begin a low, desperate moan. †

Jerry Sampson is a horror writer and screenwriter. Her love for film and the horror genre leads her to explore and question the darkness that lies in the shadows of human existence. She studies the concept of inherited trauma and finds that theme coming up unconsciously in much of her work. Jerry finds shelter in writing, reading and watching sinister stories that haunt and terrify. She lives in Portland, Oregon with her husband and cat-child.

Sean Croghan is a self-taught artist, musician, and pizza cook who thinks the three are intrinsically linked, as is his love of local mythology, natural science, and storytelling.

acknowledgements

Thank you to everyone who took a moment out of their day to read the ramblings of my somewhat odd mind. To Rich Perin for taking a chance on this unconventional storytelling and for always putting the art first in everything he does for Buckman Journal and Publishing. To Sean Croghan for finding the coolest inspiration from these stories and really putting the eerie out there for us all to enjoy. I've never seen images more relevant and ripped from the nightmares of my mind. Many thanks go to Craig Buchner and Emmi Greer for editing my stories, Ellen Robinette for handling all things illustrations, and Hannah Johnson for designing the shit out of this book. To my mom for being okay, if not slightly unnerved, with my fascination with horror early on. My ever-supportive friends Sara and Steve Dyer, Megan Calley, and of course my husband who uplifts and nurtures my creativity every moment of every day. And to my only son and feline writing companion Dante.

CPSIA information can be obtained
at www.ICGtesting.com
Printed in the USA
JSHW022055030623
42514JS00001B/69